WEIRD CONTEMPORARY FABLES

FREDERICK

BY ALVIN FIXLER

TRAFFORD   PUBLISHING

2657   WILFERT ROAD

VICTORIA, BC V9B 5Z3

CANADA

Phone: 250-383-6864

or toll-free: 1-888-232-4444

info@trafford.com   www.trafford.com

BOOKS BY ALVIN FIXLER:

RIVER RAFTING AND OUTDOOR
RECREATION GUIDE

LIVELY LATIN TALES

CONTENTS OF THIS BOOK ARE CODED
AND SEEDED FOR SECURITY PURPOSES

Order this book online at www.trafford.com/07-2784
or email orders@trafford.com

Most Trafford titles are also available at major online book retailers.

THIS BOOK IS A WORK OF FICTION. ALL CHARACTERS AND SITUATIONS ARE FICTITIOUS.

Note for Librarians: A cataloguing record for this book is available from Library
and Archives Canada at www.collectionscanada.ca/amicus/index-e.html

Printed in Victoria, BC, Canada.

ISBN: 978-1-4251-6116-3

*We at Trafford believe that it is the responsibility of us all, as both individuals
and corporations, to make choices that are environmentally and socially sound.
You, in turn, are supporting this responsible conduct each time you purchase a
Trafford book, or make use of our publishing services. To find out how you are
helping, please visit www.trafford.com/responsiblepublishing.html*

*Our mission is to efficiently provide the world's finest, most comprehensive
book publishing service, enabling every author to experience success.
To find out how to publish your book, your way, and have it available
worldwide, visit us online at www.trafford.com/10510*

 www.trafford.com

North America & international
toll-free: 1 888 232 4444 (USA & Canada)
phone: 250 383 6864 ♦ fax: 250 383 6804 ♦ email: info@trafford.com

The United Kingdom & Europe
phone: +44 (0)1865 722 113 ♦ local rate: 0845 230 9601
facsimile: +44 (0)1865 722 868 ♦ email: info.uk@trafford.com

10 9 8 7 6 5 4 3 2

WEIRD CONTEMPORARY FABLES

CONTENTS

WEIRD CONTEMPORARY FABLES

CONTENTS

CONTENTS

WEIRD CONTEMPORARY FABLES

CONTENTS

WEIRD CONTEMPORARY FABLES

A....ALARM CLOCK..An alarm clock got bored with its existence, ringing at certain times according to the way it was set.This constant,monotonous routine was affectiong it emotionally; it felt it was becoming bipolar. The alarm clock went to a psychiatrist named named Terry who happened to be a kangaroo.

Terry the kangaroo, of course, used a pouch instead of a couch for psycho-analysis. After a long discussion with Terry, the alarm clock talked about his past when he became stressed out and very woundup emotionally. Terry advised the clock to break the monotony and feel better by doing this: Ring backwards at the even number hours; forward on the odd number hours;and sideways at midnight and noon.

A....ANIMAL TRAINER..An animal trainer named Hector who was a bear had a succes-sful career training lions, tigers, and hyenas.One day he asked himself: "Hector, why are only animals trained to stand on platforms and jump through hoops in big cages? Why can't humans be trained to do

ANIMAL TRAINER..(CONTINUED)..the same things?" He consulted with his friend Rip who lived in the same condo. Rip thought carefully about the question and came up with this answer: "Humans use platforms for political rallies for one thing, and as far as jumping through hoops is concerned,there is a question as to whether or not they can be trained to do that." Hector asked if the two activities could be related. Rip shrugged his shoulders.

A....ALCHEMIST..Alchemy involves trying to turn less valuable substances into gold. An alchemist named Ambrose had four warehouses full of gold, but wanted to turn that gold into tin, because he saw all the canned foods in grocery stores. He contacted his governments Department of Alchemy, which was part of the Bureau of Unnatural Resources.

They said they were sorry, but they could only tell him how to turn tin into gold. He contacted the Department of Anti-Alchemy, which was also part of the Bureau of Unnatural Resources; they, of course gave him the same answer:

ALCHEMIST..(CONTINUED)..they could only
tell him how to turn tin into gold. He
then decided to try to sell his gold to
the government, but they said they don't
want gold----they only want tin.

A....AARDVARK..Two aardvarks were walking
down the street and saw an individual
walking on the other side of the street.
One aardvark whose name was Cyrano said
to the other one whose name was Shaw:
"Isn't that your friend George across the
street over there?"

    Shaw answered: "That's George, but he
is not exactly my friend. He was paid to
throw the Annual Aardvark Ant-Eating
Competition, and there was a lot of heavy
betting going on. Instead of losing, he
won and kept the money. He then left town
letting me hold the anthill, and confront
the angry heavy bettors." Cyrano said:
"How were you involved?" Shaw answered:
"I was his manager."

A....ALLIGATOR..An alligator named Stanley decided to go into business giving
other animals rides through the swamp on
his back. He charged five dollars a mile

ALLIGATOR..(CONTINUED)..for each ride and did very good business until he ran into a problem: A panther named Elmer hired beavers to dam up parts of the swamp and Stanley was charged a toll to go through a booth at the only opening.

He solved this problem by swapping rides for dynamite sold by lizards at roadside stands.Stanley used the dynamite to blow holes in the dams so that he could get through. He blew up all the dams and resumed business.

A....ANTIQUES..A wolf named Otto went to an antique store hoping to buy new merchandise. The antique dealer who was an armadillo named Thor explained to Otto that new items are not sold at antique stores. Otto insisted on buying a new computer operated electronic yo-yo.

Thor said he won't order or sell the yo-yo to Otto. Otto was angry and defiant with a mind of his own. He decided to open his own antique store, and got an antique store license from the city.After he was in business for awhile,he secretly bought a computer operated electronic

ANTIQUES..(CONTINUED)..yo-yo and slipped
it on to a bottom shelf of a showcase
where it wouldn't be seen. A mouse named
Timothy, who always wanted this type of
yo-yo, dragged it out on the floor and
started reading the specifications.

Just then city license inspectors
came into Otto's antique store and spot-
ted the new yo-yo. They quoted forty-
eight city ordinances forbidding the sale
of new items in an antique store and re-
voked Otto's antique store license
because he was selling one new item. They
did offer him a pet store license and
suggested that he sell Timothy, but Ott
refused to do that because Timothy was
his friend. He also hired Timothy as a
Sales Associate.

A....ARTIST..A rabbit named Amanda was an
artist who specialized in painting scenes
of pure air. She was of the Purist School
of Art , and felt that pure air was
beautiful; this meant, of course, that
there was nothing at all on the canvas.
A giraffe named Morton attending the gal-
lery showing Amanda's works mentioned that

ARTIST..(CONTINUED)..he, Morton, couldn't
see anything within the frame   of the
canvas of a particlular painting. Amanda
told Morton that time is an important
element in the appreciation of her art;
she suggested that he buy the painting
and look at it all the time for two years.

Morton bought the painting and did as
Amanda suggested; he looked at it for two
years. He still couldn't see anything so
he called Amanda and she said she would
like to see the painting at Morton's loft
apartment. She went over there and saw it
hanging on the wall. "I know exactly what
the problem is, " said Amanda. "What is
the problem?' said Morton. "You hung the
painting upside down," said Amanda.

A....ANT..A Carpenter Ant named Leon got
tired of constantly doing the kind of work
Carpenter Ants do; he became bored chewing holes in trees. He went to the Ant
Central Hiring Office (A. C. H. O) and
told them he wanted to be something else,
like maybe a Honey Ant.They told him that
was impossible because ants are born and
meant for certain roles: Carpenter Ants

ANT..(CONTINUED)..chew holes in trees, Leafcutter Ants carry pieces of leaves and flowers, Harvester Ants gather seeds, and Honey Ants collect sweet juices from flowers. Leon desperately wanted to do some other kind of work than carpenter duties. He was told that something might be done for him "under the table."

Soon he was contacted behind a tree by a shady looking ant in a black cape and black hat.They both went under a table to talk. The shady looking ant in the cape and hat was named Destin. He told Leon that for a sum of money he, Leon, could be trained for and get a job in a different ant capacity.

Leon thought for awhile and decided to do it. He contacted Destin, paid him the money, and went to the underground school to train for and become a Honey Ant. While he was in this illegal, underground school, the Queen Ant, whose name was Charlotte, found out about the illegal school and ordered the Disciplinary Ant Patrol (D. A. P.) to raid the school and arrest all the students and teachers.

WEIRD CONTEMPORARY FABLES

ANT..(CONTINUED)..Leon was taken into custody along with all the rest of the ants in the school. He was put to work chewing on the biggest and toughest trees in the jungle. Destin escaped, joined a termite colony, and ran a black market in ebony wood. There was no extradition treaty between the ants and the termites, so the ants couldn't get Destin back for prosecution.

A....AFRICA..A gazelle named Dawn got an idea for a business: She would organize a home party company to sell bananas. She went all over the jungle contacting animals to join her party plan, and signed up every animal in the jungle for hundreds of miles around.

She shipped the bananas to all the participants and they all gave parties at exactly the same time. The reason they all gave parties at the same time, was, of course, for Maximum Market Impact Within a Limited Time Frame, according to the Laws of Mass Marketing.

None of the party givers did any business at all because every one was

AFRICA..(CONTINUED)..a party giver and there were no customers to buy the bananas. Dawn had a problem. After some deep thought, she told the party givers to send the bananas back to her; after she got all the bananas back, she dumped them all on the J. B. M.(Jungle Banana Market). By doing this, Dawn introduced a new phrase into the areas of markets and investing: There are bull markets and bear markets,....now courtesy of Dawn, there is a slippery market.

A....ANACONDA..An anaconda snake named Sebastian decided to run for mayor of the jungle. A caiman named Blake also wanted that office and ran against Sebastian. They got together and talked about having a debate, and started planning the terms and rules of the debate.

These rules covered the following topics: Length of the debates, time alloted to each candidate, facilitator identity, location of debates,clothes to be worn at debates, shoes to be worn at debates, number of guests each candidate can bring,and whether the candidates

ANACONDA..(CONTINUED)..should drink tea,
coffee, milk, or hot chcolate while de-
bating.The two got so involved in setting
these debate rules that they completely
forgot about the election. The mayoral
election was won by a capybara named
Fabio who campaigned on Jungle TV on an
anti-debate platform.

A....ANTEATER..Priscilla the anteater
opened up a beauty salon called the Unbe-
lievable Dream in the jungle specializing
in permanent and non-permanent waves.
Charmaine the lioness came in one day and
said she wanted a permanent wave but
didn't have the time to get one right
then and there.

She asked Priscilla to wrap up a
permanent wave and put it in a box so
that she, Charmaine, could take it home
with her. Priscilla told Charmaine that
her request was impossible because creat-
ing permanent waves on heads is a procedure and not a product.

She said Charmaine would have to be
there in the salon to get a permanent wave
and she couldn't possibly take one home.

ANTEATER..(CONTINUED)..Charmaine became
very angry and stomped her paws on the
floor; her anger increased, and she
slapped her tail against a counter full
of baboon shampoos, gorilla styling gels,
hyema pomades,and lion mane conditioners.
"That's what I want, and I want it!" she
stormed and roared, pointing to a sign
on the wall that read: THE CUSTOMER IS
ALWAYS RIGHT!

Charmaine then called the toll-free
jungle drum number of the Jungle Consumer Protection Agency. (J. C. P. A..)
She complained to them about her problem
with the beauty salon, and that she
wanted to take home a permanent wave in
a box.

The J. C. P. A. contacted Priscilla
and told her to take an empty box, label
it PERMANENT WAVE, seal it, wrap it and
give it to Charmaine. Charmaine took the
box, smiled triumphantly at Priscilla,
pointed to the sign, and walked out of
the salon.

A....ADDAX..An addax (looks like an ant-
elope) named Homer went to look at a

ADDAX..(CONTINUED)..housing development in the desert. He found a house he liked very much; it was a quadra-level dwelling with an atrium and tower of early Cenozoic design. There was a living room; dining room; kitchen; six bedrooms; and six baths. Other features included a library, recreation room, fitness center, and swimming pool.

The development was called Sandstorm Acres, and any one buying a house there had to join the Sandstorm Acres Association.Homer asked about the benefits and obligations of belonging to the Association. He talked to the camel named Damon who was President of the Association and he told Homer there would be great benefits from being part of Sandstorm Acres development and the Association.

For one thing his lawn and bushes would be maintained on a regular basis for only a $100.00 a month assessment. Homer said I can do that myself, but Damon said that's a no-no, it must be done by the Association management. Other rules and regulations were as follows:He could only

ADDAX..(CONTINUED)..have horizontal blinds on the windows, and the slats had to be of alternating colors of blue and red.

Homer said he didn't like that color combination and Damon gave him a sharp look and said that those were the rules. There was an assessment of $100.00 a month if he wanted to put water in the swimming pool; there was also a reverse swimming pool assessment of $100.00 a day if there was no water in the pool on any given day. Tobacco use by residents was confined to wintergreen flavored snuff to be used only in the attic of the house.

Outdoor basketball hoop units on bases could be no more than four feet off the ground. Residents were permitted to have gardens as long as they only planted turnips.

Homer decided not to buy the house, thanked Damon, and started to leave the office. Damon said, "Wait a monent, please." Homer turned to Damon, and he, Damon presented Homer with an invoice.

ADDAX..(CONTINUED)..Homer said "What is this?" Damon answered "This is a consultation assessment of $100.00 for the time we spent talking about the house."

A....ALPACA..An alpaca named Simone started up her own candy manufacturing company making Andes Mountain Air Caramels. She manufactured various flavored caramels including chocolate, vanilla, strawberry, lime, pineappl, peach, apple, and lemon.

She had a staff of marmosets who answered the phones and took orders. The marmosets, called Sales Associates, took orders over the phone for flavors, packaging, weights, shipping and other details involved in ordering merchandise. A llama named Sterling who worked for a communications company told Simone that she could run a more efficient sales operation if she installed a telephone system that used menus.

Simone installed that system and when some one called to order some caramels, they would hear the following: "If you want chocolate caramels, dial extension one;" "If you want vanilla caramels, dial

- 14 -

ALPACA..(CONTINUED)..extension two;" "If
you want strawberry caramels dial extension three;""If you want lime caramels
dial extension four;" "If you want
pineapple caramels dial extension five;"
"If you want peach caramels dial
extension six;""If you want apple caramels dial extension seven;" and "If you
want lemon caramels dial extension eight."

After that, another menu would be
presented, as follows: "If you want the
caramels wrapped in waxed paper dial
extension nine;" " If you want the caramels wrapped in acetate dial extension
ten;""If you want the caramels wrapped in
cellophane dial extension eleven;"and"If
you want the caramels wrapped in tissue
dial extension twelve."

The next menu would be presented as
follows: "If you want five ounce bags
dial extension thirteen;" "If you want
ten ounce bags dial extension fourteen;"
If you want one pound bags dial extension
fifteen;" and "If you want two pound bags
dial extension sixteen."

The next menu was as follows: If you

ALPACA..(CONTINUED)..want the bags tied
with string, dial extension seventeen;"
"If you want the bags tied with a plastic
tie, dial extension eighteen;""If you want
the bags heat sealed, dial extension nine-
teen;" and "If you want the bags tied with
wire, dial extension twenty."

Another menu was as follows:"If you
want your order shipped by air, dial extension twenty-one;" " If you want your
order shipped by sea, dial extension twenty-two;" "If you want your order shipped
by truck, dial extension twenty-three;"
and "If you want your order shipped by
Vicuna Express, dial extension twenty-
four."

The menu system didn't work out well,
and Simone didn't do very much business.
Customers developed various feeling and
conditions while listening to the menus:

    ----One customer fell asleep.

    ----Another customer developed a
        nervous condition.

    ----Another customer became hypnot-
        ized and found himself repeating
        "Dial extension..Dial extension"

ALPACA..(CONTINUED)..

    ----Other customers became impatient and disgusted and hung up the phone after the wrapping instructions; they then ordered caramels from Simone's competitor, Andes Valley Caramels, who took complete orders over the phone.

A coypu (like a beaver) named Victor was CEO of Andes Valley Caramels and he offered to take over and merge with Simone but only on one condition: They would have to add a new flavor to the line of caramels: Maple. Simone agreed and became CFO of the merged companies. (CFO means Chief Flavor Officer.)

A....AARDWOLF.."Tourism could be a good and profitable business here in the jungle," said an aardwolf named Deandra to herself. She had read the best-selling book "The Romance of the Jungle or Why Does It Have to be So Noisy At Night?" by a buffalo named Brad.

    She started up a tourism and sightseeing company called Awesome Tours and

AARDWOLF..(CONTINUED)..Sightseeing. She
sold tours and sightseeing for various
sectors of the jungle, but there was a
problem: all the sectors looked alike
with trees, grass, flowers and other veg-
etation. Tour customers complained and
said the tours were boring and uninterest-
ing; they wanted tours that were fast-
paced and went to different places.

Deandra completely revised the tours
and sightseeing. She expanded the areas
and added historic buildings,non-historic
buildings, landmarks, caves, abandoned
shopping malls,and huge four-story towers.
She changed the name of her company to
"Now You See It and Now You Don't
Tour and Sightseeing Company."She planned
two basic tours: "A" and "B."

Tour A went to sixteen various spots
in the space of two days; Tour B went to
twenty-two places in four days and elimi-
minated all hotel stays, rest stops, over-
look stops, and side trips. Many tour members missed a lot of the sights because
they fell asleep, but they were happy with
the fast-paced tour they wanted.

A....AYE-AYE..An aye-aye (a lemur, looks
like a monkey) named Curtis became Water
Commissioner for Aninmalopolis, and approached the water problem of sometimes
too much water when that much wasn't
needed and not enough water when it was
needed.

The obvious solution was, of course,
reservoirs. He had a massive reservoir
built suspended above the city covering
the entire square mile area of the city.
A slight mistake was made during construction: instead of making it like a bowl to
catch and store the rain water, it was
made like an inverted bowl over the city.

Whenever it rained, instead of stor-
ing the water as it should if it was made
correctly like a bowl over the city, the
water poured over it and came down the
edges. The water poured around the peri-
meter of the construction and the peri-
meter of the city. No rain fell on the
city, but a veritable flood came down
around the city during a heavy rain.

The effect was like an enormous
"umbrella." Another problem came up: what
to do with all that   run-off water?

AYE-AYE..(CONTINUED)..The City Board appointed a Research Committee, who appointed
an Ad Hoc Committee, who appointed a Study
Committee who appointed an Investigative
Committee to look into this water matter.
Curtis was called before this last committee and asked what he was going to do
about all this excess run-off water.

Curtis said he didn't know what to do
about the problem. He was relieved of the
job of Water Commissioner, and as he left
City Hall he saw hordes of individuals
coming to the city to see the water falling around the edges of the "umbrella"
covering Animalopolis.

He ran back to the Committee and told
them of all the individuals coming to the
city to see what he called the Seventy-
Eighth Wonder of the World----The Animalopolis Umbrella. He pointed out the
economic value of the situation:He descri-
bed in glowing green terms all the money
that hotels, motels,restaurants, stores,
and other places would make from all the
visitors.

The Board definitely understood what

AYE-AYE..(CONTINUED)..Curtis meant, and following accepted procedure, voted to give Curtis his job back as Water Commissioner; after that they appointed him Mayor.

There was still the matter of the excess water, and Curtis suggested a city lottery that would pay for and build a ground reservoir. One of the Board members asked Curtis what kind of prizes would be awarded to the lottery winners. Curtis answered: "Pails of water!"

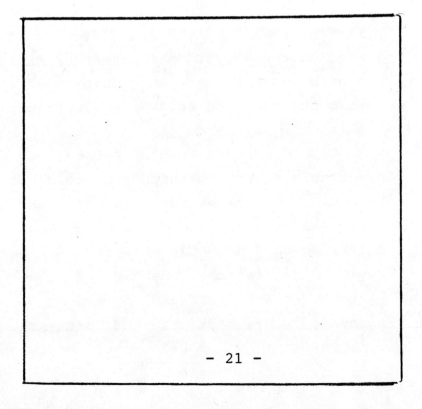

WEIRD CONTEMPORARY FABLES

B....BABY CHICK..A baby chick named
Alphonse got tired of associating with
other chicks in a barnyard. He decided
that he wanted to see the world, so he
hitched a ride on a boxcar of a passing
freight train.

He fell asleep and was awakened by
a railroad detective who was a deer named
Oswald. Oswald demanded what he, Alphonse
was doing in that boxcar. Alphonse said
he wanted to leave the barnyard and go
out and see the world.

Oswald said to Alphonse: "This is
a freight train and you can't stay on it.
I'm going to put you on a passenger train
and send you back to your barnyard."
Oswald objected and said he wouldn't go
back to the barnyard.

Oswald decided to make Alphonse an
offer he was sure to refuse: he told him
he could ride in the engine if he went
back. Alphonse countered with another
offer: he said he would go back if he
could ride in the caboose of the
passenger train. Oswald agreed and
Alphonse went back to the barnyard.

BABY CHICK..(CONTINUED)..Alphonse was
welcomed back to his barnyard with a
parade, a banquet, a presentation of the
barnyard door key, and a general celebra-
tion. He went on a lecture tour, and also
sold his story to the B. T. N. (Barnyard
Television Network.)

He also wrote for newspapers and magazines. He made enough money to be able
to buy the railroad on which he had
ridden; after he did this he appointed
Oswald to be the Security Supervisor for
the railroad.

B....BAT..A bat named Oliver grew tired
of hanging upside down. He had been hanging upside down since the day he was born
and he wondered what the world looked like
right side up.

He asked the Bat Ruler whose name was
Casper for permission to hang right
side up. Casper was horrified. He could
hardly believe what Oliver was saying. He
patiently explained to Oliver that tradition mandates that bats hang upside down,
and any bat breaking that tradition would
be exiled from the caves and have his or

BAT..(CONTINUED)..her radar jammed.Oliver, being a willful and defiant bat went ahead and hung right side up.

He did this for one day, and the next day he went back to hanging upside down. When asked why he went back to hanging upside down, Oliver said: "I get more bugs this way, and the world looks better when viewed upside down."

B....BADGER..A badger named Jay went into business manufacturing soda straws. He carefully inspected a straw and realized that straws have looked the same for many years. He wanted something new and very innovative.

He contacted a firm of management and business consultants headed by a rabbit named Liam,who did a Primary Consultation. Liam suggested a radical change in the design and engineering of the straw. He agreed with Jay that it should be some- thing different and innovative.

Liam decided on a streamlined design and in order to achieve that effect he knew exactly how to design the new straw: close each end.

BADGER..(CONTINUED)..Liam showed Jay a mock-up of the new straw design and Jay inspected it very carefully. "How does it look?" asked Liam. "Is it different and innovative enough?" "Yes it is,"said Jay. "Very different and beautiful, but there seems to be a slight problem." "What's that? " said Liam.

"How are people going to use the straw to drink liquids if both ends are closed?" asked Jay. Liam smiled and said "We will address that problem in the Secondary Consultation for the usual fee!"

B....BEETLE..A beetle named Patrick and a beetle named Mona opened up a race track to race termites. They saw termites con- suming a wooden building and noticed how fast they moved. They put an ad in the Sunday edition of the "Termite Journal" asking for termites to come to the track and race.

The ad stated that each termite would be guaranteed a minimum of a ton of high quality, maximum nourishment wood a year. Patrick and Mona were delighted to see the response, as termites crawled to the track

BEETLE..(CONTINUED)..wanting to become racers. Opening day came, and thousands of spectators and bettors crowded the grand-stand. Eight races were scheduled the first day with eight hundred and forty termites competing in each race.

The termites in each race checked the toteboard to see the odds. After that first day of racing the termites appointed a representative to talk to Patrick and Mona. The representative who went by the name of "T" told the owners that all the termite racers were retiring from racing, and were not going to race anymore.

When Patrick and Mona asked why, "T" said that the best odds that were posted for each race was zero to zero, and this was making the racers discouraged and despondent, so they all decided not to race anymore.

B....BUZZARD..A buzzard named Harry opened a florist shop and sold a wide variety of flowers and bouquets. He was doing a fair amount of business, but felt he could do better. He looked at some of the items in his condo-nest such as appliances and

BUZZARD..(CONTINUED)..noticed that they
all had guarantees and warranties of
some kind.

He started thinking that maybe he
should offer guarantees on his flowers.
He asked the advice of his wholesaler,a
chicken named Pansy. Pansy said that to
the best of her knowledge that had never
been done; she said that none of her retailers offered guarantees on flowers.

Harry was an innovative type of
buzzard and felt that since no other
floral retailer was offering guarantees
on flowers,he would make floral history
and do it.He put a sign on his shop window that read: "ALL SALES GUARANTEED.IF
YOU ARE NOT COMPLETELY SATISFIED BRING
THE ITEM BACK FOR A FULL REFUND."

Success was immediate; customers
came to his shop and his sales increased
four hundred percent.He called Pansy on
her cell phone, and, of course,she was
very pleased because he was doing so
well. But problems started coming up.

Individuals were buying flowers and
bouquets, keeping and enjoying them for

BUZZARD..(CONTINUED)..awhile, but they started bringing them back for a refund. People would, for example, keep a vase of roses on their dining room table for four months and then when the flowers wilted, they would bring them back for a refund.

Harry, being an honest retailer, of course, always honored his guarantee. Some customers were bringing back flowers that were over a year old. Harry soon had more "used" flowers in his shop than new and fresh ones.

Then another serious problem came up. Since the sign didn't mention flowers, individuals were bringing back items that Harry didn't even sell. Some of these items included toasters; coffee makers; golf clubs; car batteries; toys; saw horses; mattresses; and empty paint cans.

Harry, being an honest retailer, honored the posted guarantees on his sign. Harry was losing money, and became desperate. He called Pansy on her Cell Phone and asked for advice. Pansy, being an intelligent chicken, took Harry under her wing and told him what the basic problem

BUZZARD..(CONTINUED)..was. She told him the first thing he should do is take the "guarantee" sign down. She also told him that his idea to guarantee flowers was no good, in fact she said that the whole concept laid an egg.

B....BUFFALO..A buffalo (American Bison) named Rupert built a shopping mall that featured a kumquat store, and as far as he knew, his was the only mall with that typed of retailer. Because of that amount of exclusivity, he named his mall Squishy Mills.

The stores in the mall were doing well and the mall itself was economically viable. Parking was adequate, but not exactly great. One day Rupert was looking around his mall and saw a lot of vehicles driving around looking for parking spots.

He got an idea that he thought would benefit the patrons and make himself some money: the idea was to institute valet parking. He set aside ten spaces on the parking lot and put a sign up there reading: "VALET PARKING ONLY," and hired some drivers.

BUFFALO..(CONTINUED)..Rupert put a sign in front of the kumquat store that read: "VALET PARKING FOUR DOLLARS."A few patrons took advantage of the valet parking service, and then more and more did so.

He was doing so well with the valet parking that he designated ten more spaces and raised the price to eight dollars. His frient Lionel the squirrel told him to be careful, and that he was getting too greedy. Lionel also said that just because people liked valet parking now, doesn't mean they will always like it.

Rupert told Lionel not to be so discouraging, and that the success of valet parking would continue.Rupert added another ten spaces and raised the price to twelve dollars. The situation continued until the entire parking lot was meant for valet parking.

The day after that, Rupert went to his mall and it was empty; there were no cars anywhere on the parking lot. No cars on the lot meant no patrons at the mall, and no patrons meant no customers in the

WEIRD CONTEMPORARY FABLES

BUFFALO..(CONTINUED)..stores. The owners
of the stores got together and gave
Rupert an ultimatum: stop the valet parking or we will all move out. Rupert gave
in to their demands and cancelled valet
parking.

Rupert became nervous and stresed-
out because of all that was happening;
he sold the mall to Lionel who turned
each retail establishment into a nut
store. Rupert retired to his ranch in
South Dakota where he wouldn't hear any
discouraging words.

B....BOBCAT..A boy bobcat named Rico
loved a pretty girl bobcat named Desiree.
He continuously yearned for her and kept
going after her;he bought her flowers and
candy and even got her a stunning pink
diamond-studded ribbon for her cute short
bobbed tail.

Desiree liked Rico very much, but
decided to play the love situation cool
and act coy and hard-to-get. She felt that
this would enhance his love for her. Rico
often took Desiree to the forest drive-in
theatre to see movies and she would let

BOBCAT..(CONTINUED)..Rico hold paws with
her and let him gently stroke her tail,
but when he started to lovingly and almost
semi-passionately tweak her ears she
said "No! that's getting too intimate.
We're not ready for that yet."

Rico asked his frient Ned what he,
Ned,thought the problem was and Ned tol
him that Desiree was the type of girl
bobcat that couldn't be touched with a ten
foot pole. Rico then contacted a pole manufacturing company in the forest.He asked
them to make a custom made pole for him.
When they asked him what length, he
answered: "Eleven feet four inches long!"

B....BEAR..The Inter-Forest Games are presented each year in the forest and they
are very popular, with many participants
and spectators. Wilbur the bear was appointed Executive Director of the Games and
he worked with a Games Committee to plan
the popular event.

The games that were scheduled included croquet; marbles; trampoline; tree
climbing; vine walking; tree drumming
(woodpeckers only;) tree jumping; and

BEAR..(CONTINUED)..log rolling. The Committee started planning the preliminary
show and it was decided that a huge por-
table stage would be constructed on the
playing field. Multi-media screens would
be set up for television, film, slides,
and chalk talk.

A tableau would be used for presen-
tations in addition to singing, dancing,
acrobatics, baton twirling, fireworks,
and eagle and osprey overflying in for-
mation. Wilbur cautioned the Committee
that there may be too many preliminary
events, but they said that was no problem and they knew what they were doing.

The big day came with spectators
coming from far and near. The preliminary
show started with the how, why, when, and
who started the Inter-Forest Games; the
rules of the Games; the history of each
individual game; the names of the trees
used in the tree events; biographies of
all the past athletes for   each game;
location of all the previous   Games;
all the records made and broken for each
game; total amount of hot dogs sold for

BEAR..(CONTINUED)..previous Games; total
gallons of beer sold for all   previous
Games; and the color of the procession
uniforms worn by all participants for all
previous Games.

The Inter-Forest Games were played
in one day, and started at seven in the
morning and lasted until seven in the
evening. The Preliminary Show started at
seven in the morning and lasted until
seven in the evening and there was no time
left for the Games.

Wilbur confronted the Committee and
said: "I told you so!" The   Committee
looked at Wilbur and said that next year
they would eliminate the games and just
put on a preliminary show.

B....BUSH BABY.."Fool's Paradise" was the
name of a gambling casino owned by a bush
baby named Clarence. It was a unique kind
of casino,quite different from all others.
The winning symbol on the slot machines
was a crown,and each wheel had nothing but
crowns on it all the way around.

When individuals played the machines
they got nothing but crowns and therefore

BUSH BABY..(CONTINUED)..constantly won
jackpots. All the video poker machines
came up with maximum winnings all the
time for every one who played them.
"Fool's Paradise"soon became known as the
world's most popular casino.

The motto of the place in bright
lights in a sign over the entrance read:
"EVERY ONE A WINNER ALL THE TIME EVERY
TIME!" Individuals flocked, ran, flew,
slid, floated, descended, and used every
type of vehicle to get to "Fool's
Paradise" casino. Patrons numbered in the
hundreds of thousands.

Then, something happened. Clarence
went bankrupt.

He then reorganized his casino
company calling it "Fool's Paradise II."
He issued an Initial Public Offering (IPO)
and the pitch to potential investors was
"Invest in the worlds's most popular
casino with patrons numbering in the
hundreds of thousands!" The investors,
of course responded and bought millions
of dollars worth of stock. Clarence made
enough money to come out of bankruptcy

BUSH BABY..(CONTINUED)..and made a profit.

B....BEAVER..The idea of a new type
restaurant occurred to Montague the beaver.
He got this idea while eating at the
Forest Restaurant, and noticed that some
individuals ate their meal quickly and
some took their time while eating.

At the same time there was a long
line of patrons waiting to be seated. He
decided to start up what he called a
"Selective Express Restaurant." He would
specify certain time lengths for each meal
and let patrons choose which time period
they wanted.

There would be two time periods for
breakfast: one lasting ten minutes and one
lasting fifteen minutes.With regard to the
lunch periods, one would last twenty minutes, and one would last twenty-five minutes. For dinner one period would last for
thirty minutes and one would last for
thirty-five minutes.

An individual coming in for a meal
would have to register and fill out a
sworn affidavit that they would eat their
meal within the exact time specified for

BEAVER..(CONTINUED)..that particular sitting. A loud buzzer would sound at the end of each particular time period and the tables affected would shake. If any one went over his or her allotted time whistles, bells, screams and sirens would sound and any food still uneaten would be taken away from the table.

The offending patron would also be charged one dollar for each overtime minute. Patrons didn't like this situation at all; they didn't mind the shaking tables or the food being taken away or even the whistles, bells, or sirens, but the screams really bothered them. They didn't feel that loud screams were conducive to a peaceful and happy meal. Business at Montague's restaurant went down to practically nothing.

Montague talked to a Business Consultant and asked him what to do to get patrons back. The Consultant told him to eliminate the whistles, bells, screams, and sirens and play some beaultiful and relaxing music. This would put the patrons into a relaxed and cooperative mood and make them feel good and be more

BEAVER..(CONTINUED)..likely to finish eating within their time period and leave the restaurant.

Montague took the advice of the Consultant,but his advice was slightly wrong. True, the patrons did enjoy the beautiful and relaxing music,but they enjoyed the the music so much they stayed and ate as long as possible and paid the overtime costs. Some patrons stayed in the restaurant for days and weeks at a time,sleeping with their respective heads on the tables.

Montague sold the restaurant to the Consultant who put cots near to the tables. He knew about B & Bs----bed and breakfast establishments, and called his place E & Ss----Eat and Sleeps.

WEIRD CONTEMPORARY FABLES

C....CAT..A cat named Therese decided that she wanted to be a figure ice skater. She went to various figure skating coaches and teachers and asked them to teach her the skills necessary for that sport and art.

She always got the same answer from all of them: "Who ever heard of a figure skating cat?" She filed a formal complaint with the F. R. O. (Feline Rights Organization,) but they couldn't do anything because figure skating was not covered by their by-laws,

They told her that bowling was covered by their by-laws, and that if she should take up bowling and was denied that sport, the F. R. O. would come to her defense. Therese said no to the bowling and insisted on becoming a figure skater.

She met a coyote named Richard who was a professional figure skater, and he said he would teach her the technique provided she met a certain condition: She would only skate to music of the Neanderthal Period.

CAT..(CONTINUED)..Therese asked the reason
why, and Richard said that was his favorite kind of music.She then diplomatically
and gently told Richard that there was no
known music of the Neanderthal Period. He
said she still has to dance to that music
or he wouldn't train her in figure
skating.

Therese again appealed to the F.R.O.
and asked for help. They considered the
situation serious enough to call an international convention; after speeches,
meetings, resolutions, and discussions,
the F. R. O. told Therese that she would
have to follow Richard's orders.

Richard let out with a loud howl
of delight, but Therese said she had a
condition of her own. She wanted to skate
to a waltz. Richard agreed and booked
Therese in an ice show; she skated to rave
reviews. Since Neanderthal Period music
didn't exist, no one in the audience heard
anything at all and Therese skated to complete silence. She billed her act as the
Main Event Of Waltzing or M. E. O. W.
C....CARIBOU..Emily the caribou bought a

CARIBOU..(CONTINUED)..new appliance for her kitchen. It was a combination bread-bagel-bun toaster, and there was a control that regulated the degree of heat for whatever was in the toaster. The problem was that there was only one control on the unit, and Emily questioned whether the same settings were okay for bread, bagels, and buns.

There was an eight hundred number for customer service on the carton and Emily called them. The conversation went like this: OPERATOR: "Retsaot Toaster Company......May I help you?" EMILY: "Does the control on your toaster regulate all the items in it?"

OPERATOR: "What is your zip code, please?" EMILY:"Zero, zero, zero, zero, zero. Does the control on your toaster regulate all the items in it?"OPERATOR: "Where did you buy the toaster?" EMILY: "In a store. Does the control on your toaster regulate all the items in it?"

OPERATOR: "Do you live in a house, apartment, condo, or tent?" EMILY:"A house. Does the control on your toaster

CARIBOU..(CONTINUED)..regulate all the items in it?" OPERATOR: "What is the curren weather where you are?" EMILY:"It's raining now. Does the control on your toaster regulate all the items in it?" OPERATOR:"How often do you get a haircut?"

EMILY:"Every month. Does the control on your toaster regulate all the items in it?"OPERATOR:"Are you planning to observe the eclipse of the moon"EMILY: "No. Does the control on your toaster regulate all the items in it?" OPERATOR:"Did you ever play hopscotch on the sidewalk when you were a child?" EMILY:"No, we just played hide and go seek. Does the control on your toaster regulate all the items in it?"

OPERATOR:" What is your underwear size?" EMILY:"You tell me your underwear size and I"ll tell you mine. OPERATOR: "Sorry, our privacy policy doesn't allow us to give out that information. Thank you. Good bye" The operator then hung up.

C....CHIMPANZEE..A champanzee named Ethan bought a failing health club called the "Feelin' Good Health Club." He tried to think of ways to promote his Club and to

CHIMPANZE.... (CONTINUED)..attract more individuals; he decided that he wanted them to come on a daily fee basis.He got an idea concerning using punch cards.

He had a card printed with numbers on the edges, and each time a daily member came to the Club,their card would be punched. Once a card was filled a daily member would get a free day at the Club.

Ethan advertised on television, radio, newspapers, and direct response. The advertisng pitch was: "COME TO THE FEELIN' GOOD HEALTH CLUB! GET YOUR CARD PUNCHED FOR EACH VISIT! A FULL CARD WILL GIVE YOU A FREE VISIT FOR ONE DAY!"

But Ethan made a slight mistake: he neglected to say that a special printed card obtained from the Club had to be used. So individuals brought their own cards and flocked to the Club bringing playing cards; greeting cards; business cards; three-by-five cards;calling cards; place cards; time cards; and file cards.

Ethan knew he had a problem, and called a business consultant for advice.

CHIMPANZEE....(CONTINUED)..He told the consultant that members should use the cards from the Club.The consultant pointed out that even though individuals were using their own cards for each visit, they were still paying for each visit, thereby generating business for Ethan and his Club. The consultant also told Ethan to specify that each card had to have fifty punches to qualify for a free visit. Ethan said that's a lot of punches,and the consultant said that's also a lot of Club visits.

C....COUGAR..The Jungle Mall was a busy place when Amber the cougar visited the popular and thriving shopping center. She went to a store called the Cookie Emporium where she bought a box of"Tasty Treats"and took it home with her.

Amber, of course, read all the "Nutrition Facts"on the box before opening it; Calories: 0; Calories from Fat: 0; Total Fat: 0; Saturated Fat: 0; Trans Fat: 0; Cholestrol: 0; Sodium: 0; Serving Size: 0; Serving per Container: 0: Total Carbohydrates: 0; Dietary Fiber: 0; Sugars: 0;

COUGAR....(CONTINUED)..Protein: 0;
Vitamin A: 0%; Vitamin C: 0%; Calcium:
0%; and Iron: 0%. Amber was delighted
and overwhelmed by the sensational
health qualities of the product and she
thought that "Tasty Treats" were nutrition personified.

She was a little puzzled by the
Serving Size O and Servings per Container 0 facts, but dismissed those items as
some kind of technical specifications.
The important thing to Amber was the
immense health qualities of the cookies.
No Fat! No Cholestrol! No Sodium! What
more could an individual want in a product?

She read further: "No Artificial
Colors, Flavors Preservatives."Amber
hurriedly opened the box and tore open
the inner bag and looked inside. There
was nothing in the bag.

C....CHEETAH..A cheetah named Roderick
heard of the expression "gild the lily."
He started thinking about this phrase
and asked himself a question: "How many
lilies are there in existence that need

CHEETAH....(CONTINUED)..gilding?" The obvious answer was "Probably millions." Roderick then founded a company to manufacture materials to gild lilies and called the firm GTL Corporation.

He was about to issue an Initial Public Offering (IPO) to raise money when his friend Dax the guinea pig took him aside and explained that the phrase "gild the lily " was just that, a phrase. Dax told Roderick that lilies were beautiful flowers and didn't need any other kind of beautification.

"But, said Roderick, if the lily is already so pretty, why do I hear that saying all the time?" Dax told him that "gilding the lily" was still just an expression. Roderick was adamant about his business idea and made plans to issue the IPO.

Dax predicted that no one would buy stock in GTL Corporation but he was wrong; thousands of individuals lined up to buy into the IPO. Before any stocks were sold however, and money accepted,a problem came up. The Lily Flower Enthusiasts Society

CHEETAH....(CONTINUED)..didn't like the implication that lilies needed gilding. They said the flowers are lovely and don't need any extra decorating. The Society brought suit against Roderick and GTL Corporation and asked for an injunction to stop the company from making lily gilding materials.

Roderick thought about the situation and decided he didn't want to get involved any suit or court action. He got together with the Society and offered to dissolve GTL Corporation if the Society would withdraw the suit.

In the meantime individuals kept wanting to buy stock in GTL Corporation and the Society was aware of the great financial interest in GTL. The Lily Flower Enthusiasts Society,realizing the money to be made, called an emergency meeting of the organization.They changed their by-laws, reactivated and reorganized GTL,and bought the Company. They did, of course, withdraw the suit against Roderick and hired him as CEO.

C....COATI..Austin was a coati who liked

COATI....(CONTINUED)..to watch games and sports on television. The Jungle Spectacular Competition was the big and importan sports event of the year, and of course, it would be televised. Austin sat back in his easy chair and turned on the television to the Competition.

He looked forward to watching all the games including badminton; horseshoe pitching; marbles; high jump, broad jump; medium jump; tree climbing; tree vaulting; vine swinging; chinning on tree branches; and all the others.

The program opened with titles announcing the Jungle Spectacular Competition; after that a history of the games dating back to 22 B. C. was shown. Then histories of the three hundred and forty-two participants was presented starting from the time each participant was a child.

The camera then showed shots of the spectators; it showed separate shots of individuals, and then panned across and up and down the grandstand and bleachers. The vendors selling popccorn, beer, pop,

WEIRD CONTEMPORARY FABLES

COATI....(CONTINUED)..and peanuts were also shown as they gave out their respective products and collected the money. Other camera coverage included photographers; referees; judges; team owners; workers emptying refuse cans; workers replenishing the sand where players landed for the jump events; electricians replacing burned-out light bulbs; and custodians sweeping floors inside the grandstand.

The program then ended, and Austin had the feeling that he had missed something.He finally realized what he didn't see: the games themselves.

C....COCKROACH..A Madagascan hissing cockroach named Pico developed a bad case of laryngitis and instead of hissing , he started alternatvely rattling, whistling, clicking and groaning.

The other hissing cockroaches called a meeting and formally informed Pico that their species have to hiss,and if he didn't, he would be thrown out of the H. C. A. (Hissing Cockroaches Association.) Pico didn't know what to do until

COCKROACH....(CONTINUED)..a friend took him aside and showed him an ad in the newspaper. The ad was for a physician named Revin who specialized in hiss restoration for Madagascan cockroaches. The doctor operated on Pico and eliminated the rattling, whistling, clicking and groaning. Revin was actually a toucan.

Pico was happy about the surgery and paid the doctor for what seemed to be a very successful operation; he was,however, warned that there might be some side effects. Pico eagerly went out into the jungle looking forward to start hissing again. But, alas, poor Pico....when he tried to hiss nothing but a scream came out of him.

C....CAMEL..A camel named Ian had a strong desire to play the guitar. The more he thought about it, the more he yearned to play that instrument. When he was interviewed at the Desert Guitar Academy, he was asked why he wanted to play the guitar of all instruments.

He answered that he considered it a romantic and sensuous musical instrument.

CAMEL....(CONTINUED)..He also said he wanted to play the guitar while he was wooing Mellisa, his beautiful camel girl friend. The Academy signed Ian up for a series of guitar lessons and Ian came to each and every lesson.

In the meantime,Ian kept serenading Mellisa wherever she was--in the beauty shop getting a sand pack..while drinking her eighteen gallons of water.. outside the window of her bathroom..while getting a hump augmentation..everywhere.

One day when Ian went to call on Mellisa, he found a note on the window of her condo. The note read: "I just met a visiting guanaco named Diego from Argentina and fell madly in love with him. We eloped to his country and we plan to run together on the 10K Pampas Marathon to benefit indigent vicunas in the Andes Mountains. I got tired of that constand guitar playing----Diego plays a trombone and is a champion Tango dancer."

C....COYOTE..Penelope the coyote knew about B and Bs------Bed and Breakfast lodging places in homes. It occurred to

COYOTE....(CONTINUED)..her that some individuals might want a break or rest in the
afternoon, so she established what she
called C and Ds------Couch and Dinners.
Guests would come to her place in the afternoon, take a nap on a couch, and then
have dinner.

Penelope's idea was popular and very
successful and guests came to her C and D
from all over. Many of the guests had
such a nice time that they wanted to stay
longer; they wanted to sleep at her place
overnight and have breakfast the next
morning. Penelope said she couldn't do
that--she said if she allowed guests to
do that she would have a B and B instead
of a C and D.

She was strongly advised to open a
B and B a little way from her C and D and
she did this; guests would come to the
Couch and Dinner first, then they would
go to the Bed and Breakfast.They had such
a wonderful time at breakfast that they
wanted to stay longer, so Penelope built
another building nearby and called it an
M and N----Morning and Noon.

COYOTE....(CONTINUED)..Guests then came to the C and D, then to the B and B,and then to the M and N. The end result was that guest stayed at all three of Penelope's lodgings for a full twenty-four hours.

The CEO of a big motel chain who was a crane named Mitchell approached Penelope and made her an offer to buy her C D B B M Ns and combine all the facilities in one place. He questioned whether or not the guests liked unpacking and packing all the time.

Penelope told Mitchell that the guests didn't mind unpacking and packing because she threw fantastic good-bye parties for the guests leaving one place and wild welcome parties for guests arriving at another place. The result was constant parties which the guests really enjoyed.

Mitchell agreed to keep the three facilities and Penelope sold her places to the motel chain. Penelope was made an executive with the title of CHO--Chief Howling Officer.

D....DEER..The Royal Cart Manufacturing
Corporation was owned by a deer named
Cameron, who was President of the company.
His firm marketed a well built and quality
cart called the Monarch QK, and it was
moderately successul sales-wise.

He was working on promotions for
the coming cart model year when his Board
of Directors called a meeting, and suggested that Cameron put out other makes and
models of carts. They felt that if the
line was expanded, sales may increase.

Cameron agreed and decided that the
best and most economical way to expand
the line would be to create a new name and
make changes on the Monarch QK. He took
the Monarch QK name badge off of the front
of the cart, put a new name there and
called the vehicle a Sovereign ZL. He did
make a change: he changed the color of the
rope used to control and drive the vehicle
from black to white.

The cart went to the dealers and soon
the dealers told Cameron that there was a
great deal of sales resistance from the
potential buyers who said the cart looked

DEER....(CONTINUED)..the same as the Monarch QK. Cameron knew he had to do something, so he took the Sovereign ZL name off of the front of the cart and put a new name there: Majestic RL. He made a change, of course: he installed a square-shaped brake lever instead of a round-shaped lever.

Again, there was dealer and consumer resistance so Cameron put a new name on the cart: Prince WO, and made a change: he changed the rope fastener near the seat from a hook to a nail. Problems again from dealer and consumers, so Cameron put another new name badge on the cart: Regalia SG, and changed the shape of the headlights from square to round. The reaction was as before; sales dipped and the dealers dropped the carts from Royal and sold a competitive make.

D....DONKEY..The Spotless Carpet Cleaning Company was owned by a donkey named Chester. When he first went into business there were many homes that had carpets that needed cleaning and he did very well. But floor fashions change and

DONKEY....(CONTINUED).. other floor materials became the vogue. Chester had the
necessary equipment to clean regular
carpeting, but slate floors became the
style and he had to get the appropriate
equipment to clean slate floors.

He also changed the word "carpet" in
in the name of his firm to "floor." Soon
floor fashions changed again to bamboo
floors, and Chester had to buy new bamboo
floor cleaning equpment. Within two months
steel floors became "the thing to have"
and Chester had to buy steel floor cleaning machinery.

The situation was costing Chester a
lot of money and he did a little checking.
He found out that floor styles were being
dictated by the editor of a home fashions
magazine named Gisbelle who was a duck.
He contacted her, introduced himself and
suggested they meet for lunch at the Quack
and Paddle Restaurant.

Gisbelle agreed and they made a date
to meet for lunch. During lunch, Chester
in a diplomatic way, asked Gisbelle why
she kept changing the fashion in floors.

DONKEY....(CONTINUED)..Gisbelle answered by saying: "Fashions thrive on change!" Chester asked:"Why?" Gisbelle answered: "Things can get very boring if they always stay the same. Doesn't getting bored bother you?" Chester said: "No, spending a lot of money bothers me!"

Chester said: "I suggest you stop changing floor fashions!" Gisbelle said: "I won't do that!" Chester said:"You can only go so far with regard to floors. There is a limited amount of materials that can be used for floors, and when you've gone the limit you will have to stop! There's nothing more you can do. A flat floor is a flat floor and even you can't fashionably mandate anything different!" Gisbelle smiled at Chester and said: "Oh yeah! How about a bumpy and hilly floor!."

E ....ELAND..An eland named Julian owned a pharmacy distributorship and received a shipment of a product from a manufac-turer. The items were beautiful blue bottles with a pump on the top. The product was called ERULLA and Julian

ELAND....(CONTINUED)..delivered the items
to various drug stores who were his customers. The drug stores put the items on
the shelves and sold them to the public.
A fox named Wells bought a bottle of
ERULLA and took it home with him.

An hour later he brought it back to
the drug store and asked the manager a
question: "What do I do with ERULLA? How
do I use it?" Wells and the manager read
the copy on the bottom of the label, as
follows: "GENTLE".."NON-IRRITATING"..
"RICH".."CREAMY".."NON-GREASY".."MOISTUR-
IZES".."GENTLE".."NON-STINGING".."HYDRAT-
ING".."HEALING".

They gave each other quizzical looks.
They still didn't know how ERULLA is to be
used. Julian called the maker of ERULLA
and talked to the product manager. She
wasn't sure of ERULLA's use. In the meantime ERULLA sales were breaking records;
consumers were running to retail outlets
and buying up a couple bottles at a time.

Julian got the names and addresses of
the people who were buying ERULLA and
contacted them. They were asked how they

ELAND....(CONTINUED)..were using the product and promised discount coupons for future purchases if they responded. Julian tallied the responses and found out what the public was doing with ERULLA. The large majority answer was: As a hand lotion!. Julian sold his firm and joined the laboratory department of the ERULLA CORPORATION to develop "mystery" products for which the consuming public would find a use.

E-E....ELECTRIC EEL..Preston the electric eel supplied power to large areas of the Amazon Jungle. The current he generated was indeed unique and Preston called his power EC (Eel current), as differing from AC and DC current.

After expanding his power service to provide electricity to a new strip mall owned by a wealthy capybara,Preston decided it was time he raised his rates. He applied to the Jungle Utility Board (JUB) for a raise, and the Board called a meeting to consider Preston's request. Preston's request for a raise in rates

WEIRD CONTEMPORARY FABLES

ELECTRIC EEL....(CONTINUED)..was denied
the reason being that the Board felt
that Preston's added service didn't merit
a raise in rates. Preston got an attorney
named Stella who was a jaguar to represent
him for his appeal. They had to prove that
Preston was working harder to produce the
EC to service the needs of every one in
the jungle.

Stella was one of the toughest and
smartest JUB attorneys in the jungle. She
made an impassioned, almost semi-savage
speech to the members of the Jungle
utility Board. She spoke for one hundred
and forty-four hours straight.

There were eight members of the JUB,
and when Stella finished her speech, two
of the members were sleeping; two were
crying; two were playing canasta; and two
were getting manicures. They still said
"No!" to the raise in rates. Stella faced
them and said: "If you don't give my
client the raise in rates he deserves,
he'll leave here and go to Africa and
you won't have any electric power!"

The JUB met in emergency session and

- 60 -

ELECTRIC EEL....(CONTINUED)..decided to give Preston his raise in rates. As Preston and Stella walked away from the JUB meeting roon, he whispered to Stella "You know I can't go to Africa....I have to stay here in the Amazon Jungle!." Stella gave Preston an affectionate squeeze and said: "Don't tell that to the Board members!."

E....EAGLE..A female eagle named Brandy opened up two boutiques for women and girls selling fashions in dresses, blouses, skirts, coats, accessories,and shoes.

She called one store THE SUBLIME and the other one THE RIDICULOUS. THE SUBLIME featured high fashions at high end prices, with designs from the foremost creators in the eagle fashion world. The merchandise was shown in all the important areas of the world.

THE RIDICULOUS shop featured low fashions and low end prices. The designs were by relatively unknown individuals who created fashions in their spare time. Brandy encouraged customers to shop at

EAGLE....(CONTINUED)..both of her places, and her advertising motto was:"SHOP WITH BRANDY AND GO FROM THE SUBLIME TO THE RIDICULOUS!" For maximum efficiency, the two stores combined their computer and billing services. Brandy felt that this arrangement would simplify the billing and paying procedure.

Bills for THE SUBLIME shop would have to be paid at that store according to this schedule: From nine A. M. to noon on Monday, Wednesday, and Friday; THE SUBLIME bills would have to be paid at THE RIDI-CULOUS store between noon and nine P.M. on Monday, Wednesday, and Friday.

Bills for THE RIDICULOUS shop would have to be paid at that store according to this schedule: From nine A. M. to noon on Tuesdays and Thursdays; THE RIDICULOUS BILLS would have to be paid at THE SUBLIME shop from noon to nine P. M. on Tuesdays and Thursdays.

If customers didn't conform to this paying schedule and showed up at other times to pay, their money would be refused.

E....ELEPHANT..A cleaning, pressing, and tailoring establishment called CLEAN-LINESS MEANS HAPPINESS was owned by an elephant named Fletcher. He prided himself with regard to the work done by his place.

The cleaning and everything else was done on the premises by a staff of experienced personnel. Fletcher did well and business picked up so fast that he soon couldn't handle all the work. He decided to outsource some of the cleaning to a cleaning plant; eventually he got so busy that he sent all the cleaning there which was run by hyenas.

The work involving pressing also increased tremendously, so he outsourced all of that to a meerkat consortium composed of cottage pressing industries. The same happened with his tailoring business, which he sent to a baboon tailoring organization.

By this time there was no more work done at Fletcher's place, so all of his people went to work at the outsourcing establishments. The hyenas, meerkats,

WEIRD CONTEMPORARY FABLES

ELEPHANT....(CONTINUED)..and baboons got together and formed a cleaning, pressing, and tailoring business called H.M.B.,Inc. Fletcher still had his store fronts where customers came to leave their clothes.

H.M.B.,Inc. offered to buy the places from Fletcher, and he gave the idea some thought. One day he noticed a cart wash facility where carts went through a building in a line getting washed and cleaned. As the carts went through, hoses squirted, spigots splashed; brushes brushed; mops mopped; rags ragged; and soap outlets bubbled as the carts went along in a line.

Fletcher immediately got an idea: an elephant wash along the same lines! He accepted the offer from H.M.B., Inc. and opened up the first automatic elephant wash!

E....EGRET..An egret named Roark wanted to build a small hut where he could be by himself and just relax, think, concentrate, and meditate. He, of course, had to get permission from the Grande Wilderness Council to build this hut. There was no problem in getting a building permit, but

EGRET....(CONTINUED)..there were other
procedures that he had to go through.
After applying for and paying for the
building permit, he was given another
form to fill out to apply for an Engineering Feasibility Study.

Roark had that Study made, and it
was approved. He was then given another
form to fill out to apply for an Area
Feasibility Study. He had that Study
made and it was approved. He was then
given another form to fill out for a
Soil Feasibility Study.

He had that one made, and it was
approved. He was given another form to
fill out for an Air Purity Feasibility
Study. That was too much for Roark, and
he told the Grande Wilderness Council
members in no uncertain terms that he
had had it with Studies!

He told them that this was just a
small hut where he would only relax,
think, concentrate, and meditate. He
solemnly promised the members that he
would only think pure thoughts, and
guaranteed that those thoughts wouldn't

EGRET....(CONTINUED)..contaminate the air or harm the environment. The council asked Roark if he would swear an affidavit to that effect. Roark said he would do that, and the Council gave him permission   to build his hut.

E....ERMINE..An ermine named Ned was CEO of a manufacturing company that made a range of products including safety nails that didn't have points; damp unreuseable cleaning rags that were self-disinteg-rating, meaning they disintegrated as soon as they touched water; non-thread   drill bits with circles around the   shafts in-stead of threads; and non-abrasive sand paper with different degrees of smoothness.

Generally speaking, Ned was well-liked by all of his fellow executives; other staff members; members of the Board; and all the employees of the company. But there was something he used that no one liked: a men's cologne called Eau de Whew!!!! The unique scent of this un-usual cologne was attributable to its formulation. It was made of a combination

ERMINE....(CONTINUED)..of essential oils
and restaurant exhaust. All kinds of
messages by regular mail, E-mail, computer, and fax were sent to Ned, asking,
suggesting, begging, and ordering him
to stop using Eau de Whew!!!

Ned wouldn't give in and continued
using that cologne. The Board of Directors called an emergency meeting and
decided there was only one thing they
could do about Ned and his cologne: a
firing and buyout or a buyout and a
firing. The Board offered Ned a million
worth of stock in the company; Ned
checked the stock market information
concerning the company's stock value,
and flatly refused to take it.

The Board offered him a million
in cash, but Ned again refused. The
Board then told Ned the company would
buy him the firm that made the Eau de
Whew!!!! cologne in addition to the
million in cash. Ned was inclined to
first sniff at this offer, but finally
agreed, accepted the offer and left the
company.

E....ECHIDNA..An echidna named Tatiana owned a manufacturing company making industrial products. One of the machines in the plant broke down and an important part needed to be replaced. She contacted the company that made the part, and was told the part could only be ordered by E-mail.

The E-mail address was as follows: BBBD.com/org.wwwRTEQ.LKG./@jj.ptyrmbekud wd////&yyt/hj////re.l.p.#..com.ddfg/oouyn mkg//fewqdn/org../ohgfSA..//py#.pyerfk// lop//kkhtAAwr..////..org.

The ordering of parts was restricted to certain times in the day, and by the time Tatiana finished putting in the E-mail address, the parts department had closed. She found out the phone number of the parts company and decided to try and by-pass the E-mail address.

She called the firm on the phone and got the following recorded message: "PLEASE ORDER ALL PARTS BY E-MAIL FROM THE FOLLOWING ADDRESS...." The message then proceeded to give the long E-mail address. Tatiana then sent the parts company a letter ordering the part she

WEIRD CONTEMPORARY FABLES

ECHIDNA....(CONTINUED).. needed. She
got a letter from the company telling
her to order the part by E-mail and
giving the E-mail address. Tatiana was
desperate; she needed that part for the
machine. She made a special trip to the
parts company, went to the parts department, and tried to place an order for
the part she needed.

She was sent to a private room in
which there was a computer. There was a
card giving directions as to what she
was to do. The card read:"PLEASE ORDER
THE PART YOU NEED BY E-MAIL USING THE
FOLLOWING ADDRESS...."(The E-mail address was given.) "WE WILL STAY OPEN LONG
ENOUGH FOR YOU TO PLACE YOUR ORDER."

E....ELK..An elk named Dante owned a
store selling, repairing, and grinding
axes. One day a customer came in and
asked to have his ax ground. Dante got
into a conversation with him about politics; the customer had some very expli-
cit and emotional ideas about politics
and the current political situation.

The individual left his ax and went

ELK....(CONTINUED)..out the door. Dante
forgot to get his, the individual's, name.
Dante put the ax on a rack marked "JOBS TO
DO" with a label that said "POLITICS" to
remind him that that ax belonged to a
customer that talked about politics.

Some one else came in with an ax to
be ground and loudly complained about high
taxes. Dante put his ax on the rack and
because a personal relationahip had formed
between him and the customer, he labeled
the ax "HIGH TAXES" in addition to the customers's name.

This situation kept happening over
again, with customers commenting on and
complaining about such topics as worker
wages; the cost of food; more advantageous
trade policies; subsidies; and various
other matters. Dante got an idea to increase his business and make more money.

He put a big sign on the front of his
store that read: "GRIND YOUR AX HERE!" He
also put a sign on his window that read:
"DO YOU HAVE STRONG, EMOTIONAL, HOSTILE,
OR ARGUMENTATIVE OPINIONS ABOUT ANYTHING?
IF SO, GRIND YOUR AX HERE AND FREELY

ELK....(CONTINUED)..EXPRESS THOSE OPINIONS! YOUR COST IS ONLY ONE WILDO (WILDERNESS DOLLAR) PER MINUTE IN ADDITION TO THE GRINDING COST!"

F....FIDDLER CRAB..A fiddler crab named Kyle did all of his fiddling on the seashore and enjoyed doing this very much. Cal, his turtle friend, always listened to Kyle's fiddling and told him that he was a great musician and should play fo audiences and make some money.

Kyle thought it over and decided to do just that. Kyle performed different kinds of fiddling including classical, jazz, and other types of music. He decided he would try for classical music and went to see the conductor of a classical symphony orchestra.

He auditioned for and was led by a famous and world-renowned conductor; afterwards he sat down and talked with the conductor. The conductor told Kyle that he, Kyle, was positively great, and that he, the conductor, had never heard such polished and magnificent fiddling.

But, the famous and world-renowned

WEIRD CONTEMPORARY FABLES

FIDDLER CRAB....(CONTINUED)..conductor
said, regretfully, that he had no openings
in the orchestra for even a talented
fiddler crab. He wished Kyle the best of
luck and told him to try some other
musical orgaizations. Kyle thanked the
conductor for his time and left.

Taking the famous and world-renowned
conductor's suggestion, Kyle contacted a
jazz orchestra; a marching band; a jazz
group; and a string ensemble. They all
praised his fiddling but they all said
they had no openings. Famous conductors
with each of the above groups were very
anxious to lead and audition Kyle; none
of them had ever worked with a
fiddler crab.

But, there were no openings. Kyle
sadly returned to the seashore and met his
friend Cal, the turtle. Kyle told Cal what
happened, and casually mentioned that he
had been led and auditioned by famous
conductors. Cal looked at Kyle and said:
"Say that again....who led and auditioned
you?" Kyle said: "Famous and world renowned conductors." Cal brightened up and

FIDDLER CRAB....(CONTINUED)..said "You are undoubtedly the only fiddler crab to have been led and auditioned by so many famous conductors! This fact will certainly strike a chord with true music lovers and your popularity is sure to treble!"

Cal became Kyle's business manager and agent; he built a big, beautiful hall and charged admission for Kyle's concerts. There was literally a sand- slide of response from individuals from all over who came to hear and appreciate Kyle's fiddling. A big sign on the front of the hall read: "FIDDLING BY KYLE WHO HAS BEEN LED AND AUDITIONED BY FAMOUS AND WORLD-RENOWNED CONDUCTORS!"

F....FLAMINGO..The tree business appealed to a flamingo named Precious and she bought a lot and a building and stocked the lot with many different kinds of trees. In her advertising she stressed the importance of trees in urban and urban environments.

She was trying to think of other promotion ideas when she saw a dog chase

FLAMINGO....(CONTINUED)..a squirrel up one of the trees on her lot. The dog then stood at the base of the tree and barked at the squirrel who was up in one of the branches. The squirrel jumped from the branch of that tree to the branch of another tree, but the dog kept barking up the same tree as before.

Precious E-mailed a chipmunk friend of hers to go and tell the dog he was barking up the wrong tree, but the dog was so busy barking he didn't notice the chipmunk. Precious then got an idea: Sell a line of specialty trees for specific purposes. She put up a sign that read: " TREES FOR THE FOLLOWING PURPOSES!"....

"DOGS TO BARK UP!".."SQUIRRELS TO RUN UP!".."MONKEYS TO CLIMB UP!".."CATS TO CRAWL UP!." Very soon after she put this sign up she was visited by members of the Wilderness Committee for Correct Grammar and Language (WCCGL). They pointed to the signs and told Precious that the signs were unacceptable.

When she asked why, they told her it was because words were left without proper

FLAMINGO....(CONTINUED)..grammatical connections in a sentence. They pointed out the phrases "....bark up;" ...."run up;" ...."climb up;" ....and "...."crawl up." They told her she would have to change the signs so they would be grammatically correct. Precious asked them what they wanted her to do.

They told her to change the signs to, respectively: "TREES UNDER WHICH DOGS CAN ENJOY THEMSELVES BY BARKING!;" "TREES FOR THE PURPOSE OF ALLOWING SQUIRRELS TO ENGAGE IN THE RECREATION OF RUNNING UP AND DOWN!;" "MONKEYS WILL LOVE CLIMBING AND SWINGING THROUGH OUR TREES!;" and "CATS OF ALL SPECIES AND BREEDS WILL HAVE A WONDERFUL TIME GOING UP AND DOWN OUR TREES!."

Precious was horrified. "Do you realize what a sign like that will cost me?" she practically yelled at the WCCGL. I can't afford the cost of a sign that huge." The WCCGL members suggested that she shorten the signs to: "DOGS!".. "SQUIRRELS!".."MONKEYS!".."CATS!"

Precious told them that would put

FLAMINGO....(CONTINUED)..her into the business of selling animals intead of trees. When the WCCGL members told her to go ahead and sell animals, Precious told them she made a lot of money selling trees and questioned whether or not she could make that kind of money selling animals. The WCCGL told her to go into the animal selling business, and said they would sub- sidize her if she made less money selling animals than in selling trees. Precious agreed and opened a store selling animals. The animal store was profitable on its own so she took the subsidy money and opened another store selling trees.

F....FOX..A fox named Artemus lived in a community that was going to have an election. Candidates were running for mayor and for different city boards. One of the candidates had a personal back- ground that was somewhat shady; he had in years past done some things for which he was not proud.

When he was asked about his past, he said he didn't want to air his dirty laundry in public. Other dandidates for

FOX....(CONTINUED)..different offices
said the same thing.Artemus got an idea:
Open a laundry that will air an
individual's dirty laundry but not in
public. His or her identity would not
be disclosed.

He drove his unmarked truck to the
home of one of the mayoral candidates
and knocked on the door. The maid answered and asked what he wanted. He
said he was there to pick up the
candidate's dirty laundry. The maid said
she does the laundry in the basement of
the house.

Artemus asked her if she hangs out
the laundry in the back yard for every
one to see. The maid says she does this.
Artemus told her that what she's doing
could be dangerous because every one can
see the candidate's laundry.

The maid said the items were all
clean because they, of course, had been
washed before being hung out on the line.
Artemus told her that dirty laundry may
not actually be dirty; it may look clean
but individuals may read something

WEIRD CONTEMPORARY FABLES

FOX...(CONTINUED)..peculiar in a cand-
itate's clothing. They may look at his
hats, socks, pants, hankies, underwear,
and ties and develop some suspicious feelings towards him or her. Artemus looked
at the maid and said "Who knows what
people will think when seeing all those
intimate items waving in the breeze!"

The maid shivered, nodded her head,
and said "You're right!" Artemus told the
maid to play it safe and let him do the
laundry for a fee. He said he would guarantee that it would be hung out in private
so no one could see it.She liked the idea,
but said she would have to check with her
employer. He liked the idea too, and
awarded Artemus an exclusive franchise to
privately air dirty laundry for candidates.

F....FALCON..A falcon named Hal wanted to
put up a sign in front of his hardware
store.He contacted the Department of Signs
in his community to find out about the
rules and regulations with regard to signs.
He was given an application and a list of
sign requirements, as follows: "SQUARE

FALCON....(CONTINUED)..SHAPES....Thirty-six inches square; only black and white colors; only block lettering; and graphics only fifteen inches square.

DIAMOND SHAPES....Thirty inches on each side; only red and blue colors; only script lettering; and graphics only twelve inches square. OVAL SHAPES.... Thirty-six inch vertical measurement; only orange and green colors; only Old English lettering; and graphics only ten inches square.

RECTANGULAR SHAPES....Thirty-six by thirty inches;only pink and blue colors; only italic lettering; and graphics only eight inches square. Hal felt that these rules were extremely restrictive and asked the clerk if he had to comply exactly with all of them. The clerk said yes, Hal had to do that if he, Hal, wanted put up a square, diamond-shaped, oval, or rectangular sign.

Hal asked if there were any other rules or restrictions, and the clerk said no, no others. Hal then went and put up a circular-shaped sign in front of his store.

WEIRD CONTEMPORARY FABLES

F....FROG..Carl the frog opened a romance school to teach males and females how to attract the opposite sex. The school was divided into two sections teaching each gender their respective and proper kinds of curriculums.

Both sections had similar mottoes.For males it was:"You Can Attract More Females With Something Sweet Than With Something Sour." With females it was the same except that the word "Males" was substituted for "Females."

These mottoes were more than mottoes, they were the guiding educational philosophy of the school. Graduates of the school had to take an oath to always follow and uphold these mottoes before they were awarded diplomas.

Courses for both genders included first contact; getting better acquainted; dating; and continuing the relationship. A young ferret named Mischa took the course and as a result of what he learned at the school, met and started courting a pretty female ferret named Susannah.

Following the school's motto, he sent

FROG.... (CONTINUED)..her candy, cookies, brownies, rolls, biscuits, and breads, all of which were sweet. After sending Susannah all these sweet things for a period of time, he sensed that something was not quite right.

He finally asked her if there was a problem. She looked away from him and said: "I can't tell you!" Mischa turned her head to look at him and said: "Tell me what's wrong, Susannah!" She looked at him and said: "I don't like sweet things! I like sour things, like sour candy; sourdough bread; sauerkraut; and foods made and prepared with vinegar.!

Mischa looked at her in disbelief! He quoted the school's motto to her about attracting more females with something sweet rather than something sour. Susannah simply said she likes the things she likes!

Mischa was left with a choice: he either abides by his oath at school when he got his diploma, or breaks his oath by giving his fiancé sour foods. He asked Carl's advice about the situation. Carl

FROG....(CONTINUED)..came up with a solution to the problem. He told Mischa to enroll Susannah in Carl's school and after she graduates and gets her diploma she would, of course, take an oath to give sweet things to Mischa.

At that point Carl would absolve Mischa of his oath and allow him to give sour things to Susannah. Every one was pleased with this arrangement; Mischa and Susannah got engaged and her friends gave her a Sour Shower.They married after that, with Carl as the best frog.

G....GIBBON..The various news programs on television stations in the forest often carried stories about "closet eaters."Seth the gibbon got an idea about this group.He decided to go into business manufacturing and selling closets for closet eaters. The name of his company was Closet Eaters Corporation (CEC).

Seth planned to sell a complete line of closets: one for breakfast, one for lunch, one for dinner, and an all-purpose closet which could be used for any of the three meals. Seth advertised his products

WEIRD CONTRMPORARY FABLES

GIBBON....(CONTINUED)..extensively in
newspapers, radio, television, and by
direct response. He also put out a
catalog of his products that included
special recipes for food to be eaten
only in closets.

He got a call from a female gibbon
named Mathilde saying she wanted to
give a tea party and asked Seth if he
manufactured closets for tea parties.
Seth said no, he only made closets for
breakfast, lunch, dinner, and all-
purpose situations.

Mathilde pleaded with him to get
her a tea party closet; she said she had
already sent out invitations for the tea
party. Seth was a good and sympathetic
gibbon, and said he would make that
closet for her on a special order. He
said it would cost more than stock
closets.

Mathilde said that would be all
right and she would pay more;   Seth
started on the design and engineering
and soon produced a tea party closet
for Mathilde. Seth started thinking and

- 83 -

GIBBON....(CONTINUED)..asked himself:'How popular are tea parties? Could there be a market there?' He commissioned a research company to do a tea party survey; their results were very positive, and said ther was definitely a good market potential.

Since he had the blueprints and other material to manufacture tea party closets, he manufactured a quantity for testing.The test results were highly successful, and tea party closet sales boiled over and quickly picked up steam.

Seth, of course, added that product to his production line. He then decided to go public and registered with the Forest Securities Commission (FSC). He issued an Initial Public Offering (IPO) which did very well; the stock sold and the price kept going higher and higher.

Mathilde was a smart investor and watched the stock of Closet Eaters Corporation go steadily up and up. She organized a home party company that promoted closet tea parties in homes. Each home had to have a tea party closet in order to have a party and the closets came

GIBBON....(CONTINUED)..from the Closet eaters Corporation. Mathilde's Home Closet Tea Party Plan was very successful as more and more homes hosted the parties; the sales of tea party closets also climbed.

While all this was going on, Mathilde kept buying as many shares of Closet Eaters Corporation as she could and started an unfriendly takeover of the company. Seth was shocked to hear about this and called Mathilde. "Why are you doing this? I developed the tea party closet just for you!" Seth said.

Mathilde felt a little bad about doing this, but summed up her feelings by simply saying "Business is business even regarding tea parties!" to Seth. She told Seth she would withdraw her unfriendly takeover bid if he would spin off his tea party closet operation and let her take over and run that operation as a subsidiary. Seth would, of course, continue to make the other types of closets.Seth **agreed** to this.

GIBBON....(CONTINUED)..Mathilde still had to formally and legally withdraw her take-over bid. The Takeover Department of the Forest Securities Commission was divided into three sections: Friendly Takeovers; Unfriendly Takeovers; and Sworn Enemy Takeovers. Mathilde withdrew her bid and became CEO, CFO and CPO (Chief Party Officer) of her company.

G.... GIRAFFE..A giraffe named Mortimer decided to become a basketball player. He applied to a professional basketball team, and told them he would play fair and would only dribble and pass the ball to other players. He said he would never use his long neck to drop the ball in the basket.

The coach was somewhat surprised when a giraffe asked him to join his team and he, the coach, checked with the Jungle Basketball Association to see if there were any rules barring giraffes from play-ing basketball. There were no such written rules,but the president of the association took one look at Mortimer and made a rul-ing right then and there.

GIRAFFE....(CONTINUED)..He said Mortimer could play the game, but he couldn't use his long neck to drop the ball in the basket. This was okay with Mortimer who said when he applied that he wanted to play fair and not do that.

The coach looked at Mortimer's long neck and had visions of his team's score going higher and higher, knowing full well he would have to abide by the JBA ruling. Then he got an idea and told Mortimer that he wanted him to play a certain way: When Mortimer gets the ball he would run to the basket and hold the ball in his mouth near the basket.

He would keep his mouth open, and one of the other players would jump up and grab the ball out of Mortimer's mouth and make the basket. The coach presented his idea to the other players and asked them what they thought of putting their hand in Mortimer's mouth and grabbing the ball.

They all chorused a loud "NO!" they don't want to do it! They assured Mortimer that there was nothing personal

WEIRD CONTEMPORARY FABLES

GIRAFFE....(CONTINUED)..in their decision
and that they held him in the highest
esteem; they said he was the epitome of
potential basketball greatness. Mortimer
was disappointed and before leaving the
court he stood in the middle and slowly
turned and looked around.

The coach saw him and got an idea;
Mortimer could see and be seen throughout
the whole court and stadium because of his
long neck. The coach then appointed
Mortimer the offical cheerleader!

G....GAZELLE..Some one once quoted the
following saying to Clem the gazelle:
"Cross that bridge when you come to it."
Clem thought about this for awhile and had
certain doubts about its validity. "Why
can't individuals cross a bridge before
they come to it? " he said to himself.

This question gave him an idea:
manufacture bridges that individuals can
cross before they get to them!He contacted
a bridge building firm and had them do a
feasibility study of his idea; They said
they could design and engineer any type of
bridge to fill Clem's customers' needs.

GAZELLE....(CONTINUED)..Highway seventy-two went to a bridge called the Grand Span over the Odonogo River. Clem organized a bridge construction company two miles before that bridge; built an Adminstration Building; and put up a big sign reading: "CROSS THE GRAND SPAN BRIDGE BEFORE YOU GET TO IT AND REAP THE MYSTERY BENEFITS!" Clem used the term "Mystery Benefits" because he didn't know what those benefits are.

He felt that no one would question him about the term because of the appeal and positive connotation of the word "benefits." He thought that most individuals would say to themselves:"If the word "benefits" is mentioned, it's got to be good and right,even if I don't know exactly what they are."

Since there was no river at the site of his company he had to build the bridge over the highway. Northbound traffic was funneled to the right, then to the left over the bridge, then to the right, and then to the left onto the highway.

Southbound traffic went along the

GAZELLE....(CONTINUED)..same traffic
pattern. Clem, of course, charged a fee
for going over his bridge. A family of
chimpanzees stopped at the Administra-
tion Building and the father, whose
name was Owen, asked Clem why they
couldn't continue down the highway under
the bridge.

Clem patiently pointed out to
Owen the difference between going over
and under a bridge. He told Owen that
if he and his family went under the bridge
Clem couldn't collect the fee for going
over the bridge. Clem said the situation
would be like in reverse.

Owen thought about what Clem said,
and said to Clem: "You're right! It would
be a reverse situation which means that
if I go under the bridge you will have to
pay me the fee! Right?" "Wrong!"said Clem.
"If you go under the bridge I would consider that using the bridge twice, and you
will have to pay twice the fee!"

The situation went to binding
arbitration and the arbitrator made the
following ruling: Owen could go under the

GAZELLE....(CONTINUED)..bridge under the following circumstances:He would have to pay the fee at the point where he starts under the bridge, and then the fee would be returned to him as he left the point of coming out from under the bridg Both parties agreed and the matter was settled peacefully.

G....GORILLA..The mayor of a town was making a speech dedicating a new shopping mall called Wild Values in the jungle and it was covered on television. The Jungle Communications Commission (JCC) gave numbers to the various television stations instead of call letters.

A gorilla named lawrence was watching local TV station 0011 which was carrying the mall dedication. He decided that he wanted to see something else on the tube and switched to local TV 0022; that station also had the mayor speaking from the mall.

He continued switching, and local stations 0033, 0044, 0055, 0066, 0077, and 0088 all had the mayor's mall speech. He continued switching trying to find

GORILLA....(CONTINUED)..something other than the mall program,but distant stations all carried that event. Stations from jungles and rain forests from halfway around the world as well as one transmitting from somewhere in outer space had the same program.

He had an "Astronovision" television receiver and tuned in a station from one of the outer planets, hoping against hope that there would be something other than the mayor at the mall; no way, there was his honor still orating! Lawrence had all of the state-of-the-art technological television transmitting methods.

These included Atmospheric Television contact (ATC); Outernet Touch Transmission (OTT);Ethereal Communications Transmission (ECT); and Layered Carrier Signal Communication (LCSC.) All of them carried the mall event.

He finally got an obscure TV station number 7124 that presented a jungle soap opera called "Vines of Our Days." This story was about a company of apes that performed circus type trapeze shows out

GORILLA....(CONTINUED)..in the open in the jungle. There was so much love, affection, romance and intrigue in this soap opera that the situations amounted to "Eternal Octagons" instead of "Eternal Triangles. Lawrence was eagerly and excitedly in the middle of watching a high-flying passionate interlude in the show when it was interrupted with a momentary blank screen.

The next picture was the mayor at the mall again, and the announcer said: "We now switch you to the Wild Values mall and the mayor making a dedication speech." Lawrence angrily turned off the set.

He did very well financially in the banana distribution business and bought his own TV station. He planned all the programs himself and made sure his shows were completely different from all other stations.

His shows were so good and unique that other stations copied his shows and formats with the result being that all the TV stations carried the same

GORILLA....(CONTINUED)..presentations.
When Lawrence tuned in other stations to
hopefully see something different, he saw
what was on his station. He finally gave
up with regard to television, sold his
station to his baboon condo manager, and
devoted full time to his banana
distribution business.

G....GOOSE..The Triple and Quad Value
super market chain had many stores selling
a wide variety of food and other kinds
of merchandise. A goose named Delite often
shopped at one of these stores, but she
sometimes ran into problems.She would come
to the store, take a cart, and go up and
down the aisles getting the items she
wanted.

At the end of her shopping, she would
embark on the Great Super Market Adventure:
Find an empty (meaning no customers there)
or a comparatively empty check-out counter.
The store she was in had ten check-out
counters: Eight for any number of items;
one for ten items or less; and one counter
for zero items or less.

Delite would usually stand with her

GOOSE....(CONTINUED)..cart at the beginning of counter five and survey the check-out situation left and right. One day she looked to her left and saw that check-out counter number one was empty. She made a mad dash in that direction, but when she got there there already was fifteen people in line.

She looked far to her right, and saw that number eight counter was empty; she ran toward that one, but there were twenty individuals in line when she got there. Delite had no choice but to get in line at the end. After she paid for her items she noticed another check-out counter far off to one side of the store.

She had never noticed that one before. There was no one anywhere near that counter, no lines of customers and the clerk stood there looking bored. She went to the Customer Service counter and asked about that empty counter off to the side of the store.

The CS clerk said to Delite: "That is the Reservation Check-Out Counter." "What does that mean?" said Delite.

GOOSE....(CONTINUED)..The Customer Service
clerk said certain customers can make a
reservation to use use that counter
at a certain time, and they wouldn't have
to wait in line. "Great idea!"said Delite.
"Is there a catch to that arrangement?"
"Certainly not," said the CS clerk, acting
politely indignant.

"No catch, the clerk said, but a
certain slight requirement.""What's that?"
said Delite. "In order for a customer to
use the Reservation Check-Out Counter,
the monetary value of the customer's
total purchase must be at least one
thousand," said the clerk.

H....HIPPOPOTAMUS..Collecting rocks, minerals,and semi-precious stones was a hobby
and interest of Luke the hippopotamus. He
had been doing this for awhile on a small
scale from his home which was a condo in
a development called Imperial Hippo High-
lands on the River.Now he decided he could
do better with a retail store.

He drove around in his HSUV (Hippo
Sport Utility Vehicle) to look for a site
for his store. As he drove down one block

HIPPOPOTAMUS....(CONTINUED)..in his community he noticed a store with various rocks and minerals in the window. The sign on the building read: "ROCK." He realized that here was some competition, but knew that was to be expected.

He kept driving and passed an intersection and came to another block where there was an empty store with a sign that read: "FOR LEASE." After passing another intersection he came to a third block and saw a store with a sign on the building that read:A HARD PLACE.

There was rocks and minerals in the window of that store."More competition," Luke thought to himself. He went back to the middle block of the three blocks to the empty store with the "FOR LEASE" sign, and noted down the phone number of the lease management office.

He went back to his condo and called the number; he later met with the lease management individuals,and signed a lease. He moved into his place while trying to think of a name for his store. He noted,

HIPPOPOTAMUS....(CONTINUED)..of course, that his store was in the middle block of the other two stores, along the three block area. He again drove past his two competitors, first coming to "ROCK," and there was a big sign on the window that read: "MALACHITE..$15.00. He kept on driving and passed his store.

He then came to the other one, "A HARD PLACE," and saw a big sign on the window that read: "MALACHITE..$10.00. " He then thought of a name for his store. He put a big sign in his window that read: "MALACHITE..$5.00." He also put a big sign on his building giving the name of his store: "BETWEEN A ROCK AND A HARD PLACE."

H....HERON..A heron named Zeke was on the Board of Directors of a company called the Jungle, Wilderness, and General Product Corporation.This firm manufactured leisure environmental-friendly furniture for the home. Products included tables, dry spas, wet spas, chairs, lounges, and hammocks.

All members of the Board of Directors were also on the Boards of other companies.

HERON....(CONTINUED)..Zeke was on the Board of a company that made industrial cable. Gill the hare was on the Board of a firm that manufactured industrial pumps. A hedgehog named Fred was on the Board of a company that made steam shovels.

Dylan the hyena was on the Board of a firm that manufactured plumbing equipment. During the shareholders" meeting, a shareholder who was a hawk named Cadmus stood up and said he wanted to ask a question of the members of the Board of Directors.

Zeke said: "We welcome questions. The reason for these meetings is to get feedback from our shareholders! Ask your question please, sir." Cadmus said: "I note that you people who are members of the Board of Directors are also on the Boards of Directors of companies that manufacture products that are different and unrelated to the products of the Jungle, Wilderness, and General Product Corporation (JWGP.) What is the reason for this situation?"

HERON....(CONTINUED)..There was a full fifteen seconds of silence in the room. The other shareholders looked at each other, looked at Cadmus, looked at their respective Annual Reports, and then looked at Zeke. Zeke looked at Gill, Gill looked at Fred; Fred looked at Dylan; and Dylan looked back at Zeke.

The Directors had a fast discussion. Zeke then said:"The fact that the products of the "other" companies are different from JWGPs products instills a certain dynamism in the thinking of the Board members. That very difference regarding the products contributes to the freshness of ideas and concepts in operating the Jungle, Wilderness, and General Product Corporation.

Our Annual Report explains this concept further Every shareholder in the room immediately started to frantically leaf through their respective Annual Reports, after which they all nodded their heads in assent. They all looked at Cadmus who after a slight hesitation also nodded his head. He thanked the Board, and Zeke

HERON....(CONTINUED)..made a leisurely
but steady forecast of company earnings
for the next year. He then adjourned
the meeting.

H....HAMSTER..A hamster named Treece
decided to become a Relationship Consultant, and put out a sign in front of her
office telling of her services. A rabbit
stopped into Treece's office and told
her he needed some help regarding
a certain relationship problem.

　　She asked him about the problem,
and the rabbit told her this story: He
lived next door to a skunk and they got
along quite well, but as the skunk
passed in front of the rabbits's house,
he, the skunk, would slightly lift his
tail as if he was going to do what
skunk's do when they lift their tail.

　　However, the skunk never really did
anything. The rabbit told Treece that
this situation was making him nervous
and emotionally stressed out. Treece
told the rabbit that she would discuss
the matter with the skunk. Treece talked
to the skunk, who said he lifted his

WEIRD CONTEMPORARY FABLES

HAMSTER....(CONTINUED)..tail as a form of friendly hello. Treece told the rabbit what the skunk said, and the rabbit said he appreciated the friendly gesture, but also said he would like the skunk to show his friendliness in a different way. The skunk said he would wink at the rabbit,but that action also made the rabbit nervous.

Treece thought about the matter and came to a solution; she then called a meeting of the three individuals involved. She told them that the solution would be for the rabbit and the skunk to no longer be friends. Neither of the two cared for that idea because they liked each other as friends, but they went along with Treece.

They went to the residences of the two; their houses were next to each other, and they had adjoining lots. Treece and the two looked around the area of the adjoining lots. Treece noticed that the rabbit **had** an apple tree right at the border of the lots. Treece said; That's it!." The rabbit said: "That's what?"

Treece said: " The apple tree would be the basis for an argument, that would

HAMSTER....(CONTINUED)..effectively end the friendship between the two of you. The skunk said: "In what way?" "The argument would involve the apples falling off the tree. Note that ninety-eight percent of the apples would fall on the skunk's lot," said Treece.

"The question is 'whose apples are they?' said Treece. The tree belongs to the rabbit, but practically all of the apples fall on the skunk's property." Treece told the rabbit and the skunk to glare at each other and argue about that situation for a half hour. They did this and assured Treece that they no longer are friends.

Treece was pleased in that she had resolved the matter so well between the rabbit and the skunk. She then sent a bill to each of them for one hundred Monetary Units (MU) for her professional services. The two received the bills, but since they were no longer friends, they didn't talk to each other.

They met in their respective back yards, gathered all the apples up, and

HAMSTER....(CONTINUED)..sold them at the farmers' market in between the vehicle and storm window displays at the shopping mall. Without saying a word they split the money, paid their respective bills, glared at each other again, and went into their homes. They had nothing to do with each other after that.

K....KOALA..Rafael the koala owned a firm called Kay, Incorporated that manufactured a product in the field of technology. The product was a computer chip called a RETUPMOC that reacted to changes in relative humidity. On a scale of one to ten, the chip reacted at one during high humidity, and it reacted at ten during low humidity.

The sensor unit in the chip was a ten microtonical synthesizer with a six ZZ grid. Rafael decided to go public with his company and issued an Initial Public Offering (IPO). He contacted his many friends and asked them to buy shares; they were very interested, but would always ask about the product and wanted to know what it was and how it was used.

KOALA....(CONTINUED)..When he told them about the product they would smile, nod their heads and walk away, but wouldn't buy any shares. He talked to individuals one at a time at street corners, bus stops, restaurants, and stores but always got the same reaction: a shrug of the shoulders and: "I'll think about it," but no sales of shares.

A stockbroker friend suggested that Rafael get a storefront and sell shares from there. The friend told him to put a sign in the window reading: "BUY SHARES IN KAY, INC...MANUFACTURERS OF THE RETUPMOC CHIP WITH THE TEN MICROTONICAL SYNTHESIZER WITH A SIX ZZ GRID!"

Soon two individuals came to the front of the store and then more and more joined them; a crowd formed and that attracted more and more individuals all standing and reading the sign. They were all talking in an excited way asking each other questions such as: "Who is this company?" "What do they make?"

The answer among them was "Read the sign! It's a RETUPMOC with a ten

WEIRD CONTEMPORARY FABLES

KOALA....(CONTINUED)..microtonical synthesizer with a six ZZ grid!" Some one might
ask: "What's that?" and the answer was
"Who knows? But technology stocks are
'hot' now and anything sounding that
great and technical has GOT to be good
and make money!"

Individuals were lining up all the
way out the door of the store to buy
shares of Kay, Inc. stock. Rafael told his
friend the stockbroker that many customers
now buying shares had been contacted by
him, Rafael, previously but didn't want to
buy any before. "What's the reason for
that?" asked Rafael.

  The stockbroker smiled and said:
"Investors may act alone as individuals one
way, but if you put them in a group or a
crowd, they may act in a completely
different way. The mere fact of a crowd of
investors getting together and talking
about a stock can cause an excitement that
can become infectious!" The IPO was very
successful, and Rafael started work on
RETUPMOC 2.

K....KANGAROO..Octavio the kangaroo was

KANGAROO....(CONTINUED)..reading in his
newspaper about individuals who were
born with a"silver spoon in their mouths."
He knew, of course, what it meant: that
some one was born into wealth and
privilege. He said to himself: "Why
should only rich people have silver
spoons in their mouths? Why can't individuals in various demographic areas
enjoy silver spoons in their mouths?"

This thought gave him an idea for a
business: manufacture silver spoons for
every one to proudly buy and own! He
organized a company to do this and
called it Silver Spoons for All, Inc. He
had developed good marketing knowledge
from his former business building and
selling tree houses and tree condos to
koalas, and he knew he had tosell a complete line of silver spoons concerning
price, quality, materials and uses.

He decided to sell his spoons by
means of direct response, and took out
ads in various publications. He received
copies of those publications and while
reading one of them called the "Back-Out

WEIRD CONTEMPORARY FABLES

KANGAROO....(CONTINUED)..Journal" he noticed an ad for another company selling
gold spoons. A month later he saw an ad
in the "In-Back Magazine" selling platinum
spoons; other ads for different companies
in that same publication sold brass and
zinc spoons.

Octavio felt that this spoon idea was
his and these companies were engaging in
unfair competition. He talked to his
intellectual property attorney as to what
he can do about this situation; Octavio
suggested manufacturing a spoon with a
different design such as a square one.
His attorney said that there might be a
lot of consumer resistance to that design.

Octavio thought of other ideas for
unique spoons such as spoons without
handles;triangular ones;spoons with holes;
robotic spoons; upside down spoons; and
two-handled spoons.His attorney shook his
head and said that those spoons would
be different, but somewhat impractical

Octavio found out that all of his
competitors sold stock and were listed on
the market. He discussed the possibility

KANGAROO....(CONTINUED)..of an attempted takeover of his competitors with his corporate attorney. His attorney asked if it would be a friendly or unfriendly takeover. Octavio said it would be neither; it would be a neutral takeover.

"What do you mean by a neutral takeover?" asked his attorney."How would you do something like that?" "I would take over another company and change things about the firm,"answered Octavio. "What would you change?" asked his attorney.

"I would eliminate production of gold, platinum, brass and zinc spoons, and only make silver spoons; those firms would then become subsidiaries of my company," said Octavio. "You could do that with a friendly or unfriendly takeover," said his attorney.

"I don't want to be friends or non-friends with the other owners, I want to deal with them on a strictly business basis. Furthermore, on a friendly takeover, the executives of an opposing firm shake hands with the

WEIRD CONTEMPORARY FABLES

KANGAROO....(CONTINUED)..executives of the
other firm; on a neutral takeover the
employees of each respective company shake
hands with each other.

L....LION..Frederick the lion was driving
along a road and came to a tunnel that
went through a mountain. He drove through
the tunnel for a few minutes and saw a dim
light ahead and knew he was seeing the
light at the end of the tunnel. He got an
idea about manufacturing lights for the
ends of tunnels and mentioned this to a
friend.

His friend said that the expression
could be taken as symbolic as well as
literal, symbolic meaning an individual
striving for something that they have been
trying to accomplish for a long period of
time. When they see that light, even if
it's very small, it means that they are
coming close to what they are trying to
do. It could mean that the solution to any
problem is "up ahead."

"That's it! Frederick exclaimed. I'll
make the lights for individuals trying to
accomplish something!" Frederick got right

LION....(CONTINUED)..to work with study
and research and came up with an
ingenious light that was a combination
of ultra-violet, infra-red, gamma rays,
and brain waves from the part of the
brain that refuses to accept defeat.

Frederick started thinking about
how he was going to market and sell his
lights which he guaranteed would work
on a money back basis. His first
marketing idea concerned inventors;
he envisioned an inventor somewhere
working ona new type of machine and
having problems developing it.

He put an ad in the "Jungle
Bulletin" newspaper reading: "INVENTORS!
ARE YOU STUMPED WITH YOUR LATEST
INVENTION? BUY OUR LIGHT FOR THE END OF
YOUR TUNNEL AND SOLVE YOUR PROBLEM!" He
got a response from an inventor
developing a new type of carpet cleaner.

The inventor ordered a light from
Frederick and installed it in his lamp.
After shining the light on his invention
he was immediately able to solve his
problem and the carpet cleaner was a

LION....(CONTINUED)..huge success. The
inventor was very pleased with his light.
Frederick decided to expand his selling
efforts and started advertising to other
occupations and professions where problems
might come up.A serious moral dilemma then
faced Frederick: a criminal contacted him
and wanted a light to use for planning a
bank robbery that would be successful.

As an ethical businessman he was
obligated to sell the light to the
criminal, but on the other hand he would
be aiding and abetting a crime. Frederick
solved his dilemma by leaving one of the
components out of the light and sold that
one to the criminal. The bank robbery was
unsuccessful and didn't go off; the
criminal got away.

Frederick was afraid that the criminal
would go after him because the light didn't
work. The criminal showed up at Frederick's
office, put the defective light on the
counter and demanded a replacement that
would work. Frederick told him that he
offers a money back guarantee, but makes
no mention of replacements. He refunded the

LION.... (CONTINUED)..purchase price of the light and put the money on the counter. The criminal was very angry and accused Frederick of dishonesty; he also threatened to lodge a complaint against Frederick with the Jungle Fair Practices Sommission (JFPC). Frederick dared him to go ahead and do that. The criminal glared at Frederick, took the money and left the office.

L....LYNX..Two female lynxes named Candy and Fawn went shopping at the Forest Shopping Mall. They came into one of the entrances and entered a large,round open area; the Mall was shaped like a wheel and this open area was the "axle" of the wheel. The shopping corridors came cut of the "axle" in "spokes" and there was a total of eight main "spokes."Each main "spoke" had four "sub-spokes".

None of the main or "sub-spokes"were connected to each other. Candy and Fawn went walking down one of the "spokes" and they were just looking around at the time and not seeking anything in particular. As they walked they noticed some rather

LYNX....(CONTINUED)..peculiar scenes such as two individuals wearing large backpacks like the kind used for hiking in the mountains or the wilderness.Those two had stopped to look at large maps and charts. They also saw some one else "shooting" the sun with a sextant through a skylight and then looking at a compass.

They asked him what he was doing and he said he was trying to get his bearings. They asked "Why?" and he answered "So I can find my way out of here." They noticed a tent pitched near a pizza store, and two individuals came out of the tent in their pyjamas and went into the pizza store.

One of the bigger shops had a sign reading: "GET YOUR GPS--GLOBAL POSITIONING SYSTEMS HERE AT25% OFF REGULAR PRICE!" They stopped into that store and asked why they might need a GPS unit; they were told they might need a GPS to find their way out of the Mall.

As they walked along they came to the "Easy-Rest" Mall-Tel (as differing from a motel). They stopped in and asked the reason for a place like that at the Mall.

LYNX.... (CONTINUED)..They were told that individuals could stay at the "Mall-Tel" overnight if they got lost. Candy and Fawn did some shopping and decided to leave the Mall and go to their homes. They walked and looked around but couldn't find any exits. They were lost.

They discussed this situation with each other: How are they going to find their way out of the Mall and go home? While they were talking, Candy got an idea as she watched a uniformed custodial worker sweeping the floor and putting debris into a pan.

Candy whispered to Fawn: "That custodial worker must come from somewhere like a door possibly leading out of the Mall! Let's quietly follow her and see where she goes." Candy and Fawn followed her and passed through a Mall maintenance area with doors reading: "ELECTRIC SWITCH ROOM"; "PUMP SHUT-OFF"; and "MAINTENANCE SUPPLIES."

They also passed a door with a sign that read: "MALL OFFICE." They kept watching the custodial worker who went to

LYNX....(CONTINUED)..a door with a sign
that read: "EXIT..EMPLOYEES ONLY." There
was a keypad combination on the door and
the worker pushed the buttons and went out
the door before Candy and Fawn could get
there.

They went back to the Mall Office
door and Candy said to Fawn: "Let's go in
there and apply for a job." Fawn agreed
and they went into the office and told the
manager that they wanted jobs as custodial
workers. The manager said they didn't need
any workers at that time. Candy and Fawn
told the manager that the corridors were
very dirty and finally convinced him to
hire them.

They were hired, given uniforms, and
had their benefits explained to them. The
benefits were excellent: A very liberal
salary; a comprehensive health and beauty
plan which included health care,manicures,
pedicures, massages, haircuts, and saunas;
an excellent pension; a 401-K plan;a stock
purchase plan; vacation time; and sick
leave.

Their motive in getting the job was

LYNX....(CONTINUED)..as a way of getting out of the Mall and going to their respective homes. They planned to leave the Mall as soon as they possibly could after which they would send a letter of resignation and mail back the uniforms.

Candy and Fawn got the opportunity to leave and headed toward the exit door. Half-way to that door both of them stopped and looked at each other. They touched the Forest Shopping Mall patch on their uniforms, said "Benefits!," turned around and went back to work.

L....LEOPARD..Oscar the leopard was a television producer who wanted to come up with a completely new idea for a TV show. He thought about this constantly and especially when he was watching the shows. While he was watching a TV quiz show he realized that the usual format for those shows involved the correct answers to questions; the correct questions to answers; or a some kind of a variation of those formats.

He thought to himself: "Why not a quiz show about incorrect answers?"

LEOPARD....(CONTINUED)..He mentioned this idea to some of his associates and they laughed and said the idea was ridiculous; any one can give an incorrect answer to a question. Oscar said his idea was to give correct wrong answers and incorrect wrong answers.

Again his associates looked at Oscar, shook their heads and walked away. He decided to try and get some kind of consumer reaction to his idea and did some in-depth and scientific research. He put his idea on a flag and raised it on a tall vine on a tall tree in the jungle.

The result was very negative: not even the chimpanzees saluted. Oscar's big trait was determination and he went ahead with his show. He advertised for contestants and they were told to J-Mail (J for jungle) Oscar; eight of them wer chosen for the first show.

Oscar explained to them that there would be two types of answers: correct wrong answers and incorrect wrong answers. If they answered a question with a correct wrong answer they won a cash prize; If

LEOPARD....(CONTINUED)..they answered a question with an incorrect wrong answer, they lost.This was made clear to all the contestants and they signed papers agreeing to all these rules. The show went on the air and the contestants were given letters of the alphabet to identify each one.

To start the show, Oscar posed the following question to "A": "What is the shape of the earth?" "A" answered "Hexagonal." "Sorry, Oscar said. That is an incorrect wrong answer. The correct wrong answer is 'flat'." "A" lost.

Oscar asked "B" the following question:"What is the color of the fruit known as an orange?" "B" thought for a moment and answered: "Purple". Oscar answered "No....the correct wrong answer is 'blue'." "B" lost.

The next question went to "C:""What is the purpose of a sewing machine?""C" pondered about this question for a moment and answered:"To help navigate ships at sea." "Sorry, no, said Oscar.The correct wrong answer is: To control fireworks

LEOPARD....(CONTINUED)..displays.'"
"C" lost.

The next question went to "D":"Why do compasses point north?" "D" answered "Because the needles are out of balance." "Sorry, wrong, said Oscar. The correct wrong answer is 'Because of the influence of the northern lights'." "D lost."

"E" got the next question: "Are bananas normally peeled from top to bottom or from bottom to top?" "E" quickly answered: "The peel at the top of the banana is slightly opened and the banana is squeezed upwards out of the peel." "Sorry, you're wrong, said Oscar. The correct wrong answer is 'Sideways."E" lost.

"F" was next. The question was: "What is an unusual color for an apple?" "F" answered: "Blue." "No, said Oscar. The correct wrong answer is 'purple.'"F" lost.

The question for "G" was:"What is the shortest distance between two points?" "G" answered "A curved line." "Wrong, said Oscar. The correct wrong answer is a zig zag line'" "G" lost.

"H" got the next question: "What is

LEOPARD....(CONTINUED)..the best way to cut a head of lettuce?" "H" answered: "With a sledge hammer." "No, said Oscar. The correct wrong answer is 'With a band saw'" "H" lost.

By this time the contestants were giving Oscar some rather dirty looks, because none of them had won anything; they finally walked off the set and out of the studio.

The show, which was called the "CORRECT--INCORRECT QUIZ SHOW," soon caught the attention of the media.Words like "DEPLORABLE" and "INACCURATE" were on newspaper headlines. The president of the Jungle Educational Association (JEA) deplored and spoke out against the show saying it should be banned.

The president said the show disseminated wrong information and facts and could undermine and have a devastating effect on the entire educational system. All the members of the JEA sent Oscar J-Mails asking him to discontinue the show; they also voted to make him an honorable member if he did

LEOPARD....(CONTINUED)..this.Oscar thought about the situation for awhile and checked the ratings which were negative below negative. He accepted the membership offer from the JEA and became their Public Relations Director in charge of television.

L....LEMMING..Tom the lemming read in the "Northern Journal" about a robbery of a store after which the owner locked the door. He was reminded of the saying "To lock the barn after the horse was stolen." The owner of the store was criticized and mocked for doing this; individuals were saying that he was a little late locking the door after the robbery.

The owner, of course, defended his action saying that he had to lock the door afterwards anyway as a matter of overall security. Tom got an idea for a product from this situation: he would manufacture special purpose locks to be used only after burglaries and break-ins and things are stolen.

He would call them "Future Security TM Locks."There would be special locks for retail stores, factories, warehouses,

LEMMING.... (CONTINUED)..offices, condos, salons,, apartments, stadiums, theatres, concert halls, and convention halls. The owners of the establishments were told not to use the"Future Security TM Locks" when they built the buildings; they were only to be used after burglaries and break-ins.

If they were used improperly and put on a building when it was built and before a burglary or break-in happened, the Locks wouldn't work. The Locks also had to be used for the specific application for which they were designed and engineered; A "Future Security TM Lock" for an office building would only work on the door of an office building and not on a theatre door.

The Locks were guaranteed as long as these conditions were met; if the conditions were met Tom said he would replace anything that was stolen from a particular establishment. The Locks were what could be called "smart" (like some watches); they "knew" if they were properly or improperly installed. They

LEMMING....(CONTINUED).."knew" this on the basis of pulses they sent out to a "Future Security Dispatch Center" and all of this activity was controlled by computers.

When a dozen expensive tables were stolen from a furniture store, the "smart" "Future Security TM Locks" were installed on the doors after the theft;later another dozen tables were stolen after which a pulse was sent to the "The Future Security Dispatch Center." The tables stolen after the Locks were installed were replaced, and a truck full of tables was sent to the store.

The same thing happened when television sets were stolen a second time from apartments; the Locks sent pulses to the Center, and TV sets were sent to replace the stolen ones. Everything went well until a computer hacker found out about the Locks.

He did a few things with his computer and after a second burglary of a sporting goods store, ten cases of jock straps were sent to the symphony orchestra conductor

LEMMING....(CONTINUED)..of the concert
hall. After that the hacker sent stolen
drill presses to a theatre. This was a
serious situation that had to be
rectified. Tom gave his problem a great
deal of thought, and one day he had the
solution to defeat the hacker: Files,
file folders and telephones used by
individuals in offices.

L....LECHWE..The television set at Ryan
the lechwe's house was on and the whole
family was watching. A commercial was on
the screen. Announcer ZZ appeared with a
big smile on his face.He was talking and
saying: "THIS IS IT! A PRODUCT NEEDED IN
EVERY HOME!" The next picture showed the
following words in big letters: "FINEST
QUALITY! FINEST WORKMANSHIP! FINEST
MATERIALS! "

  The next picture showed Announcer
ZZ again saying: "THIS PRODUCT IS THE
RESULT OF YEARS OF RESEARCH! WE ASKED
WHAT YOU WANTED AND YOU TOLD US! WE'RE
BRINGING IT TO YOU NOW! The next picture
shows an automatic machine filling
moving bottles but not showing what is

WEIRD CONTEMPORARY FABLES

LECHWE....(CONTINUED)..being put into the bottles. The word "FAST!" is flashed on the picture over the bottles. The next picture shows a huge industrial stamping machine in action with the following word in large letters: "EFFICIENT" on the picture.

An automatic moving bag-filling machine is shown next, not showing what is being put in the bags. The words "TIME SAVING!" is on the picture. An unmarked semi truck is shown next with the word "ECONOMICAL!" flashed on the truck.

Announcer ZZ came on the screen again and said with a smile: "LISTEN TO THESE TESTIMONIALS!" Individual "A" appeared on the screen and said "I WAS NEVER ABLE TO UNTIL I STARTED USING THIS PRODUCT!" Individual "B" was shown next: "MY PANTRY SHELF WAS AS SOON AS I STARTED USING THIS PRODUCT!"

Individual "C" appeared on the screen and said:"MY GARAGE DIDN'T UNTIL I STARTED USING THIS GREAT PRODUCT!NOW IT DOES!" Individual "D" was shown next who said: "THE ATTIC OF MY HOUSE WAS THERE ON THE

LECHWE....(CONTINUED)..DAY I STARTED
USING THIS PRODUCT!." Announcer ZZ came
on the screen smiling, and said: "THIS
PRODUCT IS GUARANTEED TO FROM THE DAY
YOU BUY IT AND IF YOU ARE NOT SATISFIED
THAT'S FOR A LONG PERIOD OF TIME! BUY
IT AT YOUR LOCAL STORE!"

Ryan turned to his wife and said:
"What is it!." His wife turned to the
children and said :"What is it?. "The
children turned to the dog Odif and said
"What is it?! Odif didn't answer. Ryan
shrugged his shoulders and switched
channels to the "Jungle Quiz" where the
contestants were asked questions that
had no possible answers.

M....MEERKAT..It was election time in the
jungle ! There were many candidates for
all the offices and they were campaigning
by using all media including television.
Norm the meerkat and his wife Thelma
turned on their TV set and sat back to
hear one of the candidates making a
speech.

An individual appeared on the
platform and started talking: "I STAND

MEERKAT....(CONTINUED)..BEFORE YOU AS A CANDIDATE COMMITTED TO SERVING YOU TO THE BEST OF MY ABILITY! I AM COMMITTED TO SERVING YOU IN A WAY THAT WILL BE HIGHLY BENEFICIAL TO EVERY ONE!" Thelma turned to Norm and said: "What office is he running for?" Norm said: "I don't know. I'm sure we'll find out later in his speech."

The candidate continued: "I AM PROUD OF MY PREVIOUS RECORD BUT I WILL NOT SIT BACK ON MY LAURELS BUT STRIVE EVEN FURTHER TO MAKE MY SERVICES A MODEL OF EFFICIENCY AND MANAGEMENT! I WILL BE ACCOUNTABLE TO EVERY ONE REGARDING MY HONESTY AND INTEGRITY!"

Thelma turned to Norm and said: "He sounds great! Do you have any idea at all as to what office he is running for? Norm answered: "No, but he certainly is good!" The candidate continued: "I ASK YOU TO LOOK AT MY RECORD! FIND OUT ABOUT THE THINGS I HAVE ACCOMPLISHED! BUT IF YOU ELECT ME I WILL DO MORE, MUCH MORE!

I WILL ELIMINATE ALL TAXES! I WILL ESTABLISH BONUSES AND GRANTS FOR EVERY ONE! THERE WILL BE FREE TUITION FOR ALL

MEERKAT....(CONTINUED)..COLLEGES AND
UNIVERSITIES! ALL SPORTS AND RECREATION
FACILITIES WILL BE FREE TO EVERY ONE!
"Did you hear that? " said Norm. "He's
the one that should be elected!" "For
what office?" Thelma almost yelled.

"Who cares?" said Norm. "Listen to
those glowing promises! Don't you want
the things he is promising?" "Sure,
said Thelma. But he still might be
unsuitable for whatevery office he's
running for!" "We'll find that out after
he gets that office if he is elected,"
said Norm. "But that's not very logical,"
said Thelma. "No, but that's politics,"
said Norm.

M....MONGOOSE..Samantha the mongoose was
asked about suspension bridges by her
daughter Brisa. Brisa wanted to know the
length of the longest suspension bridge
in the world; she needed this information
for school.

Samantha turned on her computer to
get this information and put the
necessary data in. She got the following
on the screen: "BRIDGE..RAILROAD: A

MONGOOSE....(CONTINUED)..platform that is used to support signals over a track." She tried again and got: "BRIDGE..METALLURGY: Firebrick on a metallurgy furnace." She tried again: "BRIDGE..ANATOMY: The upper line of the nose." Again: "BRIDGE..GAME: A popular card game."

Again: "BRIDGE..MUSIC: A support that raises the strings of a musical instrument above the sounding board."She tried again: "BRIDGE..NAUTICAL:.A platform from which a power vessel is navigated."Brisa said: "Forget it, Ma! I'll get the answer some other way!"

Determination was one of Samantha's primary qualities and she said to Brisa: "I'll get the answer from that computer or else....! And she glared directly at the screen! She again put the data into the computer and got:"BRIDGE..DANCE: A rooflike figure formed by dancers by joining and raising hands."

She tried again:"BRIDGE..ELECTRICITY: A measuring device for resistance" Samantha glared at the hard drive and th screen and tried again: "BRIDGE..BILLIARDS:

MONGOOSE....(CONTINUED)..Arch formed by
the fingers and hand that supports and
guides the striking end of the cue."
Samantha was getting a little disgusted
and frustrated, but she tried again and
got: "BRIDGE..BUILDING TRADES:A scaffold
built to protect pedestrians during
construction." Samantha turned to Brisa
and said: "I'm glad we saved and still
have that set of encyclopedias!"

M....MONKEY..Alana the monkey was a very
health conscious individual and she
read all the health sections of magazines
and newspapers. She also listened to the
radio and watched all the health programs
on television.

While watching the popular "Swing
For Your Health" on television the host
of the show said: "THE LATEST STUDIES BY
THE FOOD THINK TANK GROUP HAVE SHOWN THAT
STEWED CANAFLANS ARE VERY BENEFICIAL TO
AN INDIVIDUAL'S HEALTH! THEY SUPPLY
EVERYTHING A BODY NEEDS FOR STRENGTH AND
ENERGY!"

This was enough for Alana; she
went to the Super Jungle Mart and bought

MONKEY....(CONTINUED)..ten cases of stewed canaflans. A week later she watched the same program on television and the host said: "WE HAVE JUST HEARD THE LATEST NEWS CONCERNING STEWED CANAFLANS. BE VERY CAREFUL OF THEM, AND DRASTICALLY REDUCE CONSUMPTION! THERE HAVE BEEN REPORTS OF SOMEWHAT PECULIAR AND MYSTERIOUS SIDE EFFECTS FROM A MYSTERIOUS INGREDIENT!"

Alana was surprised to hear this, but kept her stewed canaflans and didn't eat any. A week later she watched the same program and the host said: "IF YOU WANT TO STAY HEALTHY EAT AT LEAST FOUR STEWED CANAFLANS A DAY! LATEST TESTS SHOW THAT EVERY ONE NEEDS THIS FINE FOOD! BE SURE TO INCLUDE THEM IN YOUR DIET!."

A week later she watched the same TV show and heard the host say: "WE HAVE SOME DISTURBING NEWS ABOUT STEWED CANAFLANS! DON'T EAT THEM! REPORTS ABOUT THEM AND THE EFFECTS THEY CAN HAVE ON THE BODY HAVE NOT BEEN GOOD! THE MYSTERIOUS INGREDIENT IN THEM HAS BEEN IDENTIFIED AS A MYSTERIOUS INGREDIENT BY SCIENTISTS!

THIS INGREDIENT HAS CAUSED MYSTERIOUS

MONKEY....(CONTINUED)..SIDE EFFECTS THAT
ARE BEING INVESTIGATED AND IDENTIFIED!
A CALLBACK IS IMMINENT!

M....MANDRILL..It was Vine Awareness
Week in the jungle as declared by the
Vine Promotion Council and Taylor the
mandrill was having a great time looking
up at all the events and ceremonies. As
he enjoyed himself he got an idea: The
idea was to start a business that would
create awareness programs.

He felt that private individuals
should be able to declare and enjoy
awareness feelings and emotions and share
those feelings and emotions with others.
He decided to call his company Awareness,
Inc. He put an ad in the "Jungle Journal"
that read: "YOU TOO CAN ENJOY AN
AWARENESS EPISODE! CELEBRATE YOUR FINEST
MOMENTS BY MAKING EVERY ONE AWARE OF YOUR
HAPPY FEELINGS! CALL AWARENESS, INC. AT
1-XXXX-YY.

Taylor got a call from an impala
named Smith who bought a new door mat and
was proud of it. Smith asked Taylor if
his new door mat was important enough for

MANDRILL....(CONTINUED)..an awareness program. Taylor assured him that it was of great importance. He told Smith that door mats have graced the doors of great and famous individuals through the ages. He said that kings, queens, rulers,presidents, emperors, and prime ministers have wiped their respective shoes,slippers, sandals, and maybe bare feet on door mats before entering castles, palaces, great houses, and mansions.

"Really?" said Smith,and wiped a tear from his eye. Taylor started the awareness program by sending notices to the major media including the internet.The awareness program was wildly successful in the jungle and individuals came from far and near to see and marvel at Smith's door mat.

Television stations sent mobile crews as did all the leading radio stations and the Drum News Service. Smith's home and property were mobbed by eager individuals wanting to see and celebrate the famed door mat.

Cartgate parties were held on Smith's

WEIRD CONTEMPORARY FABLES

MANDRILL....(CONTINUED)..front lawn and
tents were pitched in his back yard.The
results of Smith's awareness program
became overwhelming and out of control.
Smith told Taylor that he, Smith, was
going to do something about the problem
and Taylor told him to go ahead and do
something.

Smith looked in the pink pages of
the Jungle Bushathon Directory under
"Publicity Reversal Companies" and found
a company called Unawareness, Inc. He
called them and talked to the CEO who
was a gnu named Jake. Jake started his
company because he realized that there
was a need for unawareness companies to
deal with situations that went to far and
got out of hand.

Smith asked Jake if he could help
him and Jake said he could. The first
thing Jake did was to approach Smith with
an offer he could refuse to buy the door
mat. Smith was to say the least
surprised,and said "But I'm your client!"
Jake made another offer Smith couldn't
refuse.

WEIRD CONTEMPORARY FABLES

MANDRILL....(CONTINUED)..Jake bought the
door mat from Smith and had it designated
a collectible because of all the fame it
had achieved during its awareness period.
Jake then sold it to an auction house that
specialized in awareness collectibles
where it was auctioned off for a great
deal of money. Taylor made the highest
bid and bought the door mat.

N....NIGHTINGALE..Katy the nightingale was
wandering through a shopping mall and saw
a sign on one of the big anchor stores.The
sign read: "GOING OUT OF BUSINESS SALE!"
YOU CAN BUY MERCHANDISE 'FOR A SONG!" Katy
went into the store and found something
she liked and needed.

She stood in front of the item,
pointed to it, and started singing. After
she finished singing she asked the clerk
to wrap it up for her. She took the parcel
and walked away. The clerk said: "Wait a
minute. You have to pay for that
merchandise." Katy smiled and said she did
pay fo it by singing and referred the
clerk to the sign that said: "merchandise
for a song!"

NIGHTINGALE....(CONTINUED)..Katy went to another counter and found something else she needed. She burst into a different song than the previous one and after she finished she asked the clerk to wrap the item for her. The clerk knew what had happened before and told Katy she had to pay for the item first.

Katy laughed and said "Read your sign! I just sang for it!" By that time two security individuals were standing near Katy. One of them said: "You will have to pay for the merchandise" Katy said: "Look at your sign! It says 'Buy merchandise for a song.'"

The security individual said:"That is just a figure of speech. It doesn't really mean that you can get products by just singing. You still have to pay for things you want." Katy sang in her most beautiful mezzo-soprano: "No way!" She was gently ushered into each of a number of offices where she was told she has to pay for the merchandise.

These offices included: "CUSTOMER SERVICE,""CONSUMER RELATIONS," "LOSS

NIGHTINGALE....(CONTINUED)..PREVENTION"
"ENVIRONMENTAL RELATIONS," "MISCELLANEOUS
RELATIONS," and "CONSUMER RESOURCES." Katy
kept refusing to pay and told all the
managers to look at their own sign. The
managers of all the departments had a
meeting and decided for the sake of good
will and public relations to let her have
the items without paying.

They quietly whispered to Katy that
she could have the merchandise without
paying this time, but only this time.
Another customer overhear the whisper and
that whisper turned into other whispers;
soon every one in the store burst into
song and walked out with free merchandise.
The sign came down immediately after that.

O....OKAPI..Candace, who was an okapi,
owned a nursery where she sold all kinds
of flowers, plants, bushes, and trees.The
sign at the entrance to her place read:
"DON'T LET GRASS GROW UNDER YOUR FEET!"
She chose this fairly common saying
which was rather odd for a nursery,because
she felt it would attract attention and
add a bit of humor to her establishment.

OKAPI....(CONTINUED)..Candace decided to
sell her own brand of grass seed and
further extended the humor of her sign;
she called the seed "WON'T GROW UNDER
YOUR FEET GRASS SEED." She had a company
customize the formula and manufacture the
seed and told them to make sure that the
grass would only grow in the proper
places.

The manufacturer made a mistake when
they developed the seed, and the seed
caused grass to grow under the feet.This
was okay as long as individuals walked
on their lawns that were sowed with the
seed, but some of the seed stuck
to their shoes and when they walked
somewhere else, grass would grow.

Grass grew when they walked into
their homes;lawns developed in hallways,
living rooms, dining rooms, bedrooms,
kitchens, and bathrooms of their houses.
The seed was of a very tough and hardy
variety that had been exposed to a strong
carbon dioxide/Gamma Ray effect and the
roots were able to penetrate any kind of
flooring.

OKAPI....(CONTINUED)..Homes were quickly being transformed into lawns and vacuum cleaner manufacturers were hurriedly developing in-home lawn mowers Most individuals, however, missed their tile, hardwood, parquet, and carpet floors and didn't like grass taking over the rooms of their homes.

Candace started an immediate recall of the grass seed when she heard what was happening, but many homes were full of grass by that time.Home owners got together and demanded to know what Candace was going to do about the grass in homes situation. She told the home owners to mow the lawns in their homes and send the clippings to her after which she would give all of them a full refund of the money they spent on grass seed.

All of the home owners did this except a wealthy chimpanzee family who lived in a huge tree mansion. They realized the potential sightseeing value of a home with lawn floors and put up a big sign reading: "COME SEE THE ONLY HOME IN THE JUNGLE WITH LUXURIOUS LAWN FLOORS!" They , of course,

OKAPI....(CONTINUED)..charged a moderate admission fee to go through their home and made quite a lot of money.

O....OWL..Monty, who was an owl, was a professional photographer and had a great deal of experience taking photos of individuals and groups. As he looked at all the framed photos of clients in his studio he noticed something: Every one in all the photos was smiling.

He asked himself a question: "Why was everybody smiling?" The obvious answer was: "Because they want to smile and this is the way photos are taken." Monty, who was a bit of a rebel, and sometimes defied convention, felt that things don't always have to be done the same way.

He put a sign in the window of his studio that read: "FROWNING PHOTOGRAPHS TAKEN." He got quite a bit of response and questions were asked as to what the sign meant. Monty explained that every one in photographs seem to be smiling and he thought that there may be individuals who would rather frown when photographed.

OWL..(CONTINUED)..Monty got quizzical looks as if individuals were thinking: "Are you kidding? Every one smiles when their photo is taken!" Then, one day Dean the gopher came into Monty's studio and quietly said he would like to take a frowning photo.

"Are you sure you want to do this,?" asked Monty. "Yes, positive," said Dean with averted eyes. "You will have to go to counselling first," said Monty. "Okay, I'll do that," said Dean. "You will also have to sign a release," said Monty. "A release for what?" asked Dean. "A release to absolve me of any liability," said Monty.

"What do you mean?" asked Dean. "Even though I carry malpractice insurance, I still have to be very careful of law suits," said Monty. "You may some day regret having that frowning photo taken." Dean thought for a minute and said "Okay, I'll sign the release." Dean made an appointment to take the frowning photograph and Monty prepared the studio scene.

When Dean came for the appointment,

OWL..(CONTINUED)..Monty asked him what degree of frown he preferred. Dean asked Monty how many degrees of frowing there are. Monty told him there were four degrees available for the photograph: A light frown;a medium frown;a "grayish" frown; and a very dark frown. Monty said the frown should match Dean's mood at the time the photograph is taken. Dean chose the medium frown.

Dean was posed by Monty and they were about ready to take the photo when suddenly the door to the studio opened. Two representatives of the Forest Smile Society presented Monty with a court order to stop him from taking photos with subjects frowning. Monty asked why they were doing this.

They told him that frowning photos were prohibited because they might promote mass melancholy among individuals and cause pessimistic thoughts. Monty cancelled the appointment with Dean and promised to only take smiling photos in the future.

O....OPOSSUM..Sales at the Kleenemup

OPOSSUM..(CONTINUED)..Vacuum Cleaner firm
were not doing well at all.The line on the
Sales Graph in the Sales Department was
straight for awhile, then increased
slightly, then went straight and then went
way down. The CEO of the firm, an opossum
named Barney, called a meeting of the vice
presidents of the various departments
including Sales, Production, Marketing,
and Advertising.

He told them that something has to be
done to increase sales; he also told them
that he doubts if the company will meet
the expectations of the analysts at the
"Forest Financial Journal." He also told
them he has an idea that he strongly feels
will increase sales. He told them of his
idea, as follows: "As you all know, the
trend in advertising and sales promotion
is to target the individual consumer and
build up a profile of the individual to
whom we want to sell our product.

We must find out as much as possible
about the consumer and every charactistic
is important. Rather than 'scatter' our
promotion shots in a manner of speaking

OPOSSUM..(CONTINUED)..we must pick out and find the consumer that will compare our vacuum cleaner against our competition in a store, point to the Kleenemup and say: 'That's the vacuum cleaner we want!'" The Vice President of the Sales Department asked Barney how he was going to do this.

Barney answered:"We have retained a research company to do some market research and they will tell us who is likely to buy our product. A month later Barney called a meeting of all the vice presidents and told them about the research results.

He spoke to the group and said:"As you all know, we have four models of our product, and I will tell you the Target Profiles of our customers for each of the models on the basis of the exhaustive research. These profiles are as follows: Basic Kleenemup 10....Target Profile AA: Female, weighing from one hundred and ten to one hundred and twenty pounds; partially clothed when doing housework; likes rock-and-roll music; and favorite

OPOSSUM..(CONTINUED)..flower is the rose.
Power Kleenemup 20....Target Profile BB:
Female, weighing from one hundred and
twenty-one to one hundred and thirty
pounds; almost semi-partially clothed
when doing housework; likes violin music;
favorite flower is the daisy.

Extra-Power Kleenemup 30....Target
Profile CC:Male,weighing from one hundred
and thirty-one to one hundred and forty
pounds; pumps iron at a health club;likes
march music; favorite tree is the elm. Our
Super-Power 40....Target Profile:Male DD,
weighing over one hundred and forty pounds;
works out at a boxing club; plays jazz on
a tuba; favorite tree is the oak.

These are the Target Profile buyers,
the consumers that will buy our vacuum
cleaners. The vice presidents looked at
each other for a few seconds but didn't
say anything. The Vice President of Sales
raised his hand. "Yes," said Barney. The
Sales VP said: "Barney, how are all these
characteristics related to buying vacuum
cleaners? Why would a one hundred and ten
pound female who likes rock and roll music

OPOSSUM..(CONTINUED)..want to buy our Basic Kleenemup 10 vacuum cleaner rather than a vacuum cleaner model from the competition?" Barney smiled and said: "Because that's what the research says!"

There was silence again as the VPs gave each other searching looks, and after that they all looked at Barney. Barney then said: "We have to do things according to the research and make our plans on the basis of the various Target Profiles for each of our models. As I told you each of our models has a Target Profile and the consumer of each respective profile will buy the model that is assigned to them.

"What do you mean 'assigned?'" said the VP of Advertising. "It simply means that the consumer has to buy the model in his or her Profile category," said Barney. "<u>Has</u> to buy that model?" said the Production VP. "Suppose the Target Profile individual in one category wants to buy the cleaner in a different Target Profile category?"

WEIRD CONTEMPORARY FABLES

OPOSSUM..(CONTINUED).."They can't do that,"
said Barney. "The retail stores selling our
vacuum cleaners will be notified as to
which Target Profile individuals will be
allowed to buy which models. There has to
be a correct match; each Target Profile
will be allowed to buy only the model that
goes with it. This is the way we
keep control of our marketing.

The Target Profile/Kleenemup vacuum
cleaner promotion campaign started. After
two weeks Barney got a call from one of
the retail dealers with a problem.
A female, matching Target Profile AA
wanted to buy the Kleenemup Model 40 that
matched Target Profile DD. The dealer, of
course, refused to sell it to her, telling
her that she had to buy the Basic Model 10
that matched her Target Profile."

The female became very angry and
insisted on buying the Super-Power Model
40. When the dealer still refused to sell
that model she threatened to take the
company to court to force it to sell her
the model she wanted. Calls came in from
many other dealers with the same problem:

OPOSSUM..(CONTINUED)..consumers were
refusing to adhere to the Target
Profile/Kleenemup Model matchups. Soon
a large group of consumers got together
with an attorney and started procedures
for a class action suit. The four vice
presidents called an emergency meeting
with Barney and pointed out the serious
situation the company was in.

They were not only facing a law
suit, but they were also losing many
thousands of sales. They said that the
Target Profile/Kleenemup Model matchup
rules had to be cancelled to allow any
consumer to buy whatever cleaner model
he or she wanted. Barney was adamant,
however, and insisted that things would
work out eventually and the promotion
would be successful.

The four vice presidents knew they
had to do something before the company
went out of business or bankrupt. They
called a secret meeting at which they
discussed serious actions to take to
try to get Barney out of the company.
Some of these discussed alternative

OPOSSUM..(CONTINUED)..actions included firing Barney, but he had a contract. They also thought of resigning from the company and then attempting an unfriendly takeover. While they were talking about the situation, news came that the consumers who brought the class action suit against the company had won their suit.

The judge ruled that the company had to sell whatever cleaner model any consumer wanted regardless of that consumers Target Profile, or even if they didn't have any kind of a Target Profile. Thousands of consumers flocked to retail stores to buy Kleenemup cleaners and the factory had to go on a twenty-four hour shift to produce enough cleaners to meet the tremendous demand.

The sales chart zoomed up to the ceiling in the Sales Department, and the company's earnings and profits kept increasing. Kleenemup Company stock was considered Value stock and the P/E ratio was low. A banquet was held and Barney was showered with honors, including the privilege of not making a speech, a gold

OPOSSUM..(CONTINUED)..watch,a handshake, and a bonus.

O....OSTRICH..An ostrich named Riley owned a firm called the Imperial Never Stop Growing Grassmat Corporation. He decided to run a sweepstakes to help publicize his company and boost sales. The company manufactured mats made out of grass.

Riley created a set of rules for entering the Grassmat Sweepstakes, as follows: NO PURCHASE NECESSARY. A PURCHASE WILL NOT ENHANCE CHANCES OF WINNING BUT WILL BE APPRECIATED AS IT WILL INCREASE SALES OF THE COMPANY. The Sweepstakes will begin AT 12:01 P.M. Central Jungle Time on August 25 and end at 12:01 P.M. Central Jungle Time on September 29. All entries must be postmarked by September 29.

ELIGIBILITY: In order to enter the Sweepstakes an individual must be a native resident of the Planet Earth.They must reside in a house with a minimum valuation of 20,000 in Correct Currency. The house must have a mimimum of six

OSTRICH..(CONTINUED)..rooms, a slate roof, a minimum of eight windows, and be completely free of termites. ENTERING SWEEPSTAKES: Any of the following methods can be used to enter the Sweepstakes:Mail, jungle drums, Outernet, Intranet, Jungle Mail (J-Mail,) or Elimiscaf (Facsimile spelled backwards to protect privacy.)

PRIZES: First Prize is a full, solid, complete, square Grassmat measuring ten miles on each side. A hundred other prizes are full, solid, complete, square, Grassmats measuring five miles on each side. Company will pay for Grassmat delivery any where within two blocks of the factory.

LIMITS OF LIABILITY: The Imperial Never Stop Growing Grassmat Corporation disclaims any and all responsibility for any consequences of the use of their "Never Stop Growing" Grassmats. This Disclaimer covers all acquisitions of "Never Stop Growing" Grassmats.

WINNERS OF GRASSMATS: If a winner's Grassmat grows too far and too fast, he or she may enter the Limit Grassmat

OSTRICH..(CONTINUED)..Sweepstakes where winners of the Grassmat Sweepstakes can win prizes telling them how to curb the excessive growth of a winning Grassmat. "Excessive growth" is defined aa a Grassmat covering one or more counties in a state.

P....PENGUIN..Chantal the penguin heard two of her friends talking about their dreams and ambitions, and one of them responded to the other by saying:"That's pie in the sky!" This remark gave Chantal an idea: Bake and sell pies in the sky! She built a pie bakery on the top of a tall building complete with ovens and a retail store to sell the pies.

  While she was making these plans a friend of hers who happened to be a business consultant asked her if she thought customers would go to the top of a tall building to buy her pies. Chantal said she thought they would if her pies were tasty and delicious. She said consumers will go to great lengths and maybe even heights in the pursuit of

WEIRD CONTEMPORARY FABLES

PENGUIN..(CONTINUED)..quality. The pies were outstanding and Chantal was busy baking and selling them at her store on the twentieth floor of a building. She called her business "Pie In The Sky!" and put a bright sign on the building. She was very successful.

Chantal had a supposed friend named Lanee who was also a penguin, and envious of Chantal's success with her business. Lanee looked up at the "Pie In The Sky" sign at the top of Chantal's business building and thought to herself: Why should people have to go all the way to the top of that building, a total of twenty stories, to get some pie?

Lanee opened a pie bakery and retail store on the ground floor of the same building occupied by Chantal. She called her business "Pie on the Ground Floor!" Her pies were also very good and she did a good business, taking away some of Chantal's customers.

Chantal was furious and consulted with her attorney about taking legal steps against Lanee. Chantal's attorney filed a

PENGUIN..(CONTINUED)..legal suit with
regard to the situation, which involved
Unfair Pie Marketing Practices against
Lanee. Lanee, in turn, sued Chantal on
the grounds of a Free Market Pie
Economy. The case went before a judge
who studied it very carefully, looking
for precedents regarding former pie
marketing litigation.

The judge decided on a compromise
settlement and called Chantal and Lanee
to his courtroom. He looked at both of
them as they stood in front of the
bench. His ruling was as follows: Each
would open a branch retail store on the
tenth floor of the building where they
both now had businesses.

The stores would be at opposite
ends of the building. Chantal would only
sell cream pies and Lanee would only sell
fruit pies; this arrangement would go on
for six months and after six months they
would switch pie types. The judge felt
that this arrangement would give both
parties equal slices of the pie business.

The ruling turned out to be

PENGUIN..(CONTINUED)..what was called a non-landmark (because it involved a building) case for the judge. It equaled a former case concerning a round/square pie design infringement case in which the same judge ruled.

P....PELICAN..Gary the pelican was told by a friend of his who was going to take a test that he, the friend, was burning the midnight oil. This happened in a society where oil was used for lighting. This gave Gary an idea: manufacture oil for different time periods and he opened a business to do this.

Gary called his basic product TIMELY OIL with additional names for various time periods.TIMELY OIL was very successful and sales of the product went very well. Users sent Gary letters of appreciation for his product and testimonials, saying he could use the testimonials in his advertising.He decided to do this and put the following testimonial in an ad in the "Swamp Journal:"

"From a user :'I baked a cake at four P. M. using ordinary oil in my lamps and

PELICAN..(CONTINUED)..the cake fell when
I took it out of the oven. The next time
I baked a cake at four P. M. I
used TIMELY FOUR P. M. OIL. The cake
rose to a full height of twelve inches!
TIMELY OIL is absolutely wonderful!'"
Another user wrote: "I did my laundry
at eleven A. M. using ordinary oil in
my lamps.

The clothes didn't come out very
clean at all and the colors were bad.
The next time I did laundry at eleven
A. M. I used TIMELY ELEVEN A. M. OIL
and my laundry came out very clean with
pure whites and brilliant colors!TIMELY
OIL is terrific!"

An individual in the business world
wrote: "I had an important meeting at two
P. M. and used ordinary oil in the lamps.
The meeting didn't go very well, and I
wasn't able to close a very important
deal involving a large sum of money.

I scheduled that same meeting again
at two P.M. the next day and used TIMELY
TWO. P. M. OIL in the lamps. The meeting
was very successful, we closed the deal,

PELICAN..(CONTINUED)..and our company made a lot of money! TIMELY OIL is great!" An artist wrote: "I was painting a picture for an art show, but I was not satisfied with it. I kept changing it, revising it, adding to it, and taking elements away from it.

I finished the picture, entered it in the show, but didn't win anything.I always start painting at twelve noon. I bought some TIMELY TWELVE NOON OIL and started painting another picture. When I finished it, I knew it was good. I entered it in a show, and won first prize! I owe it all to TIMELY OIL!"

Gary sold shares in his Timely Oil Company through Imperial Swamp Investments and Brokerage.Timely Oil was considered a Growth stock with a usually high P/E ratio; financial analysts gave Timely high ratings. A private investment group headed by a pelican named Chance became interested in Timely and contacted Gary and asked if they could meet.

Gary agreed and they scheduled a meeting at four P. M. on a thursday at

PELICAN..(CONTINUED)..a conferance room at the Timely Company offices. A maintenance individual at the offices filled the lamps in the conference room with ordinary oil in preparation for the meeting with the investment group.

Gary was gettting some papers together for the meeting when a thought came to him and he glanced up at the lamps. He picked up the phone and made a quick call to the maintenance department.He asked what kind of oil was in the lamps in the conference room.

He was told ordinary oil was in the lamps. He looked at his watch and noticed that there was only two minutes before the meeting. He ordered TIMELY FOUR P.M. OIL for the lamps immediately; the oil was rushed to the conference room and put in the lamps. Right after the lamps were filled, and the workers left the room, Chance and his associates entered the room.

The meeting was held and within an hour Gary sold his company for exactly what he wanted for it. After all the

PELICAN..(CONTINUED)..papers were signed,
Gary looked up at the lamps full of TIMELY
FOUR P. M. OIL and murmured "Thanks!"
Chance asked Gary who he was talking to,
and Gary answered "Uh..the lamps!" Chance
and his associates gave each other puzzled
looks, and left the room.

Gary used the money to buy himself a
private marsh, lagoon, and an island on a
lake where he engaged in team fishing with
other pelican friends. As Gary enjoyed
himself and thought about his business
deal to sell his company, he quietly said
to himself: "That was a real scoop!"

P....PARROT..Eduardo the parrot was
working on a project with some other
individuals and problems came up regarding
inportant matters. A meeting was held to
discuss the problems and then to finally
come to a conclusion concerning a solution
that would be compatible to all concerned.

There was extended conversation,
debating, arguing, and commenting, much
of which didn't really address the source
of the problems. The meeting clearly was
not getting anywhere. Finally one of the

PARROT..(CONTINUED)..individuals became very exasperated and said: "Let's get down to brass tacks!" Another member of the group said:"That's a good idea! The best idea we've had so far!"One of the members of the group was sent to a hardware store to buy a pound of brass tacks; he brought them back to the meeting and put them on the table in front of every one.

They discussed the problems further and within an hour they found a solution and finished the project to every one's satisfaction. Eduardo thought about what happened and the phrase "Let's get down to brass tacks" kept running through his mind.

He was convinced that the brass tacks led to a solution of the problems that confronted his group. He was also sure that other groups could benefit from the right kind of tacks. He decided to go into business manufacturing tacks made of different materials such as platinum, gold, and silver as well as brass. The different kinds of tacks

PARROT..(CONTINUED)..would be marketed for occasions and situations other than jus meetings. They would be promoted as a way of insuring that things would go well and problems would be solved whatever the circumstances.

To insure accuracy, tacks of certain materials could only be used for certain purposes, and Eduardo invented a machine called the Conversation Infusion Injector (CIJ). This machine was used in the manufacture of the tacks. The CIJ would cause individuals using specific tacks to talk according to the purpose and the classification of the tacks.

Platinum Tacks would only be used for board meetings of corporations capitalized at over ten million dollars; Gold Tacks would only be used for corporations capitalized at under ten million dollars; Silver Tacks would only be used for various personal occasions and events such as weddings, reunions, anniversaries, parties, celebrations, conventions, etc., etc. The Brass Tacks would only be used for all other occasions and events.

PARROT..(CONTINUED)..The business went
very well for Eduardo and his sales and
profits steadily increased, but one day
there was a mixup in the shipping
department. Platinum Tacks ordered by
the ABC Corporation that were supposed
to be sent there, were mistakenly sent
to an Award Party and Tournament of
poker players.

Silver Tacks meant for the poker
players were sent by mistake to the
Board of Directors of ABC Corporation.
When the President of the poker players
group opened the box of Platinum Tacks
the first thing he said was: "I'm glad
to report an increase in profits for
our company!"

The other players put their cards
down and gave each other puzzled looks.
One of the players said to the President:
"What are you talking about?" The
President looked confused and said: "I
don't know!"

One of the players whispered to the
one next to him and said:"I think there
is something wrong with regard to those

PARROT..(CONTINUED)..tacks!" The other one
said: "You're right!" At the Board of
Directors meeting at ABC Corporation, the
CEO opened the box of Silver Tacks and
placed it on the table in front of all the
members. He then said: "I'll take four
cards!"

The other members of the Board looked
at the CEO, looked at each other, and then
shook their collective heads. One of the
members whispered to the one next to him
and said:"It must be the tacks!" Both the
CEO and the President of the poker
group contacted Eduardo and demanded to
know what happened with the tacks mixup.

Eduardo apologized to both of them
and asked each what kind of an adjustment
they wanted. The poker group President
and the CEO got together to discuss the
matter. The CEO played a little poker now
and then, and the poker group President
always had an ambition to run a big firm.

They decided to switch places: the
CEO would join the poker group to improve
his game and the poker group President
would learn how to be a CEO.

P....PRAIRIE DOG..A prairie dog named
Kavita went to the cleaners to drop off
an item of clothing to be cleaned. While
she waited,an individual in front of her
was complaining because his coat wasn't
ready when promised.

He argued with the counter worker
and was quite angry. The counter worker
apologized, but the complainer was still
angry and getting angrier. The counter
worker then said: "Are you going to make
a mountain out of a molehill?" The
complainer vehemently said: "Yes. That's
exactly what I'm going to do!" There was
almost a slight hint of pleasure in his
voice.

Kavita thought to herself: "There
may be many individuals who would like
to make mountains out of molehills! I
could make a sport and game out of that
idea!"She modified the idea somewhat,
realizing that it would be difficult
for individuals to actually make
mountains so she defined "mountain" as
a high hill. She kept the word "mountain"
though, and the high hill would be higher

PRAIRIE DOG..(CONTINUED)..than a molehill.
Kavita put an ad in the "Wilderness Times"
that read: "HAVE YOU EVER WANTED TO MAKE
MOUNTAINS OUT OF MOLEHILLS? YOU CAN DO IT
NOW! COME TO KAVITA"S MO-MO RECREATION!"

She bought a large lot and hired
twenty moles to make hills. A pile of dirt
and a shovel was on a rack near
each molehill. Participants paid ten
dollars to go to a molehill and use the
shovel to make a "mountain," a high hill,
that is, near the molehill.

They had fifteen minutes to do this.
A prairie dog friend of Kavita came by
"KAVITA'S MO-MO RECREATION." He asked her
what the point was of this mountain-out-
of-molehill sport and game. She said there
is no point to the game.

Her friend then asked Kavita why
individuals came to her place to play the
game.Kavita pointed to the sign at her
place and said:"Read it!" The sign read:
"COME TO KAVITA'S MO-MO RECREATION TO
PLAY MAKE A MOUNTAIN OUT OF A MOLEHILL!"
"But why do they come here to play the
game?" asked her friend. Kavita answered:

PRAIRIE DOG..(CONTINUED)..Because I tell them to do it with my sign! Many people will do as they are told without asking any questions. They read my sign and do what it says! Kavita was very successful with her business, opened branches, and later sold franchises.

P....PANDA..A candy factory manufactured various kinds of taff   and the candy was made on a vertical machine which was called   a   Taff   Order,   Technical, Automated, Mechanical unit.The shortened name of the machine was TOTAM, and it was often called a pole--a TOTAM POLE.

The machine was as high as a two-story building and eight workers   ran the operation. There was one on top; one down from there; one down from there; one down from there; one down from there; one down from there; one down from there; and one at the bottom. The one at the bottom was the low worker on the TOTAM POLE.

A panda named Lace was the owner of the   business   and   she   supervised   the

PANDA..(CONTINUED)..operation of the TOTAM
POLE machine. Lace had problems. None of
workers wanted to be the low worker on the
TOTAM POLE. It was not just a matter of
prestige, although that was a factor. What
they didn't like about being low worker on
the TOTAM POLE was that all the other
workers looked down on him.

Lace first tried to solve the problem
by eliminating the low worker. This turned
out to be impractical, to say the least;
once she eliminated the low worker, there
was always one above there who turned out
to be that low worker. When she eliminated
that one, there was another low one above
that.

As she kept eliminating workers, she
finally had no workers left. She then
re-hired all of them and tried to solve
the problem another way. She put a
circular opaque shield around the pole
just above the low worker so he couldn't
be seen by any of the others above him.

This wasn't a good idea either,
because the morale of the low worker went
even lower because he got lonely and felt

PANDA..(CONTINUED)..that he was an outcast. Lace talked to a Business Consultant and he suggested eliminating the poles so that the machine was built horizontally along the level of the ground. Lace did this and thought that her problems were over with this new twist in her taffee operation.

Her problems were not over. There was still a beginning and end with the taffy making process, and the man at the end complained just like the low worker on the TOTAM POLE.

Lace decided to avoid the sticky situation with the taff and looked into the manufacture of other kinds of candies. She chose to make multi-flavored jelly beans, and assigned each worker to make a separate flavor, and by doing this she eliminated any kind of personal competition.

P....PORCUPINE..The headline on the front page of the "Forest Journal" read: "HUGH GGGGGG IN THE LIMELIGHT AFTER WINNING THE ELECTION!" Corky the porcupine read the headline and got to thinking about the

WEIRD CONTEMPORARY FABLES

PORCUPINE..(CONTINUED)..word "limelight." He knew what it meant: Some one in the public view to whom every one was paying attention. The individual would be important or feel important. Corky had a hunch that maybe light itself might have that effect on people.

He decided to start a company that would manufacture lights and, of course call them limelights. Corky became CEO and CFO of his firm. He put an ad in the "Forest Journal" that read: "YOU TOO CAN BE IN THE LIMELIGHT! BUY OUR 'LIMELIGHT MODEL 24' AND SHINE IT ON YOURSELF TO FEEL REAL IMPORTANT!"

He realized that he may be making a somewhat shaky claim for his product, but felt that individuals would gain a lot of self confidence from using his light.After many limelights were sold, Corky got a letter from a consumer that read: "My name is George and I worked for a company for ten years and never got a raise. I bought your 'Limelight Model 24' and let it shine on me everyday for eight hours for a full week. The next day I walked into my boss's

- 170 -

PORCUPINE..(CONTINUED)..office and I
demanded a raise. My salary was
quadrupled. I owe it all to your great
light!" A plumber named Goran wrote to
Corky saying he only worked on plumbing
jobs in small houses and bungalows. He
said he was always afraid and hesitant
to go after jobs in bigger dwellings.

He felt that something was holding
him back, not letting him connect with
his real plumbing skills. He bought the
'Limelight Model 24' and let it shine
on him for ten hours every day for six
days. Immediately after that he felt
infused with ambition and pressured with
confidence!

He went after plumbing jobs in big
houses, huge mansions, condos, and
high rises! "Thank you 'Limelight Model
24' for what you did for me!," he wrote
to Corky. Corky was, of course, pleased
with these and similar letters; sales
and profits for his company increased.

Corky assumed that if the product
he was now selling--'Limelight Model 24'
--had such a great effect on individuals

PORCUPINE..(CONTINUED)..that other types
of lights would do the same. He decided
to create a line of lights based primarily
on his 'Limelight Model 24.' He created
the following line:'Orangelight Model 32';
'Lemonlight Model 54'; Applelight Model
72'; and 'Nectarinelight Model 84.'Corky
presented his line idea to his Market
Research Department for evaluation.

Corky realized that he would have to
expand his company to produce the new line
of lights, and that the expansion would
cost a great deal of money. The Market
Research Department called a private
meeting without Corky, and after a few
giggles and snickers and whispered words
about 'fruit stands,' they called Corky
into the room.

They told him that they don't
recomment he go ahead with his idea of
expansion regarding the different types
of lights. The Vice President of th
Department told that the sales potential
for the new lights was very low, and the
tooling costs to produce them was very
high, too high. Corky, however decided to

PORCUPINE..(CONTINUED)..go ahead with his idea for a line of lights. He was asked if he knew whether or not the new line of lights would have similar effects on individuals as the limelights did. Corky answered by saying that he assumed that the new lights would have similar effects as the 'Limelight Model 24' light.

The Marketing staff told him that it is dangerous to base marketing decisions on assumptions, and that those decisions should be based on facts and not hunches. Corky scheduled a meeting with the Board of Directors, but when he got to the door of the Boardroom, the door was locked and he didn't have the key.

He hired a friendly beaver to chew around the lock and pushed the door open. The Board Members glared at him and they all chorused a loud "No!" There was a violent argument and all the Board Members refused to go along with Corky's idea.

He gave some thought as to what he

PORCUPINE..(CONTINUED)..could do and came
to a solution: he was already Chief
Executive Officer (CEO) and also Chief
Financial Officer (CFO). He appointed
himself Chief Decisions Making Officer
(CDMO.) As CDMO, he could rule over every
one and ordered plans to be made
for expanding the line of lights.

The company went ahead and marketed
and sold the line of lights, and Corky
was right when he said the new line would
have similar effects as the 'Limelight
Model 24.' Sales and profits doubled and
tripled and Corkey's company was voted one
of the five thousand best firms to work
for in the forest.

When Corky was interviewed for a
profile article by an editor of the
"Forest Business News," he was asked about
his decision to expand the line of lights.
He quoted the following sales adage: "When
selling something to a consumer, one does
not say 'Do you want to buy this?' but
rather 'Which do you want to buy?.'"

P....PLATYPUS..Tawny the platypus was
watching television with her family and

PLATYPUS..(CONTINUED)..a commercial came on the screen for the ACME TOASTER OVEN. The commercial was comparing the ACME product with a competitor called the MONARCH TOASTER OVEN. The two products were shown side by side on the screen.

The announcer first talked about the ACME TOASTER OVEN: "This is the ACME TOASTER OVEN, the Toaster Oven you need, you want, and must have! It is not just the 'state of the art' in ovens....it is beyond that! It will meet and exceed all your needs and expectations!

Look at all these sensational features: An automatic bread type recognizer; a ten way toast ejector; an on/off/pause/hesitation switch; and a robotic toast server. The ACME TOASTER OVEN is the oven for you!

Now look at the MONARCH TOASTER OVEN." The announcer then frowned, gave an almost semi-sour look at the MONARCH, and gave the same look into the camera. "Good? Maybe but....who knows? Features?" A hesitating, questioning "Yeah? An electronic bread type recognizer; a

PLATYPUS..(CONTINUED)..a slant/vertical/
horizontal/angular toast ejector; an
on/off/pause/reverse switch; and a manual
transverse toast server. Features?" The
announcer grimaced at the MONARCH and then
into the camera. He then shivered.

"Now let's go back to the good one--
the ACME TOASTER OVEN! " He pointed to
the ACME." This is undoubtedly the oven
you should buy!" Tawney's daughter Yolie
turned to her mother and said:"We need a
new toaster oven mom."

Tawny answered: "Yes, we do need a
new one and we're going to buy one."Yolie
said:"We'll get the ACME, I suppose. I"m
sold on this commercial for that Oven!"
Tawny said:"No,dear.We'll get the MONARCH!"
"But this commercial is for the ACME.They
did a good job of selling me on the ACME!"
said Yolie."This is a great selling TV
commercial." You're right,"said Tawny.
It is a great selling commercial and they
sold me on the MONARCH!"

P....PEACOCK..Two individuals were talking
near where Uma the peacock was standing.
She heard one of them say: "You can't have

PEACOCK..(CONTINUED)..your cake and eat it too." The other said: "Why not?" "Because you can't, the first one said. That's all there is to it." "That's not fair. said the second one. Individuals should be able to have their cake and eat it too."

Uma agreed with the second one and gave the matter some deep thought. While she was pondering the situation she decided that she should buy a bakery and sell cakes; she felt that by doing this she would be led to a solution of "Having one's cake and eating it too."

She completely remodeled the bakery and gave it a name: "That Takes the Cake Bakery." Just before the grand opening of her establishment Uma got an idea about the cake situation: She would sell two lines of cakes consisting of one line called the "Have Your Cake and Eat It Too" series and a "Not Have Your Cake and Eat It Too" series.

If customers wanted to buy a "Have Your cake and Eat It Too" series cake, they would pick one out, pay for it, and

PEACOCK..(CONTINUED)..take it home and eat it. If they wanted to buy a "Not Have Your Cake and Eat It Too" series cake, they would pick one out, pay for it and leave it at the bakery without taking it home and eating it. When Uma went to the weekly meeting of her poker club, she was asked if any one bought the "Not Have Your Cake and Eat It Too" series of cakes.

She answered:"Of course not.Why would any one want to buy a cake, pay for it,and then not take it home and eat it?" She was then asked why she sells the "Not Have Your Cake and Eat It Too" series if no one buys those cakes. Her answer was: "Because that series highlights and helps promote the "Have Your Cake and Eat It" series.

Customers sometimes laugh at me for offering both series, but then they do consider both series and think to themselves: "I want to have my cake and eat it too" so they buy a cake in that series. They end up happy and I end up with a sale.

Q....QUAIL..A cleaning and pressing

QUAIL..(CONTINUED)..establishment called
the Etamitlu Cleaners (ultimate spelled
backwards) was having problems with its
equipment and some of the clothing they
cleaned came out unsatisfactory. Many
of the customers complained about the
work they did and said their items were
no cleaner than when they turned them in
and that some were dirtier.

The President of the company, a
quail named Ignatius,installed brand new
equipment and offered to re-do the items
of unsatisfied customers at no charge.
He issued a publicity release to the
"Forest Review" newspaper concerning his
offer in this regard.

The paper published the following
headline on the front page of an issue:
"ETAMITLU CLEANERS TO MEND FENCES BY
RE-CLEANING CLOTHING!" Right after that
issue of the paper came out, Ignatius
got a phone call from some one named
Laurent who said he was a customer who
got back dirty clothes, and that he also
had a wooden fence that needed mending.
Ignatius told Laurent that he will be

QUAIL..(CONTINUED)..glad to re-do his, Laurent's,clothes and make them perfectly clean, but that Etamitlu Cleaners doesn't mend fences.Laurent said that the headline in the paper said that Etamitlu would mend fences.

Ignatius explained that the phrase "to mend fences" was a figure of speech-- a metaphor--and was not to be taken literally; Etamitlu was a cleaning company and didn't mend fences. He told Laurent that in his, Ignatius' case, "mending fences " meant that Etamitlu was going to make things right and please all the customers.

Laurent became very angry and hostile and threatened to take Ignatius to court and sue him if Etamitlu didn't mend his fence. Ignatius in desperation called the Ecnef Srednem Company (fence menders spelled backward) and talked to them about mending Laurent's fence.

Before he actually engaged the Ecnef company, he called Laurent and told him that Laurent's clothes would be cleaned free of charge, but that there would be

QUAIL..(CONTINUED)..a charge for mending
his fence. Laurent said that was okay,he
would pay the cost.Ignatius called Ecnef
and asked them for the cost of mending
Laurent's fence; staff of the Ecnef firm
drove past Laurent's place and looked
at the fence through binoculars and
determined the cost of mending it.

Ecnef told Ignatius the cost and
he marked it up a very fair two
hundred percent, and then told Laurent
the cost. Laurent okayed the price and
told Ignatius to go ahead with the
fence mending process. In the meantime
other customers of Etamitlu were calling
wanting their fences mended.

Soon Ignatius was doing more fence
mending business than cleaning and
pressing; he then made the Ecnef firm
an offer to buy that firm, which they
accepted. Ignatius kept his cleaning
and pressing business and offered
free cleaning and pressing with every
fence he mended. After taking a mesure
of his profits, he later addded a free
tailoring service.

R....RHEBOK..Hudson was a weathy rhebok
who made his fortune in the jungle options
exchange. He always had an idea to buy and
own a restaurant; he bought one and wanted
to make it unique and different from other
eating places. He was watching a televison
cooking show and the chef was singing to
himself as he was preparing a dish.

Hudson got an idea: let the patrons
of his restaurant sing for their food. He
called his place the "Sing For Your Supper
Restaurant." Hudson made plans with regard
to the singing feature of his restaurant
and decided to do the following:As patrons
entered they would either go to an open
area and sing to every one in the dining
area or they could go to a private
soundproof booth if they wanted to sing
privately.

The customer would be given two
minutes to sing; the singing was judged by
a Music Panel appointed by Hudson. The
criteria was simple: Acceptable or
Unacceptable.The Panel met in secret in a
back room of the restaurant.

The customer would then be seated and

RHEBOK..(CONTINUED)..he or she would wait for the singing judgement and in the meantime would choose their food from a menu. If a patron's singing was judged acceptable, they would get their food for a minimum amount and the tip.

If the patron's singing was judged unacceptable after he or she chose the food from the menu, they would have to pay the cost of the food but they wouldn't be allowed to eat it. Hudson's cousin Craig came to Hudson's restaurant often and noticed the many customers whose singing was unacceptable who had to pay the cost of the food they weren't allowed to eat.

Craig opened up a singing school across from Hudson's dining place and put up a sign that read: "LEARN TO SING HERE AND BE RATED ACCEPTABLE AT THE'SING FOR YOUR SUPPER RESTAURANT'ACROSS THE STREET!'" Craig did very well with his singing school and the graduates were getting acceptable ratings and getting the food at very low prices.

Hudson was also happy because the

RHEBOK..(CONTINUED)..customers were singing acceptably and buying the food; the food was cheap but Hudson made up for it because of the volume.Hudson made Craig and offer to buy into the singing school and Craig agreed and sold Hudson a forty percent share in the school.

Soon the Authorities notified Hudson that he couldn't own shares in the singing school and also operate the restaurant; there was a conflict of interest.They told him that his restaurant and the singing school were not in harmony with jungle anti-trust laws.

Hudson sold his shares in Craig's singing school and opened up his own singing school.Since this was Hudson's own, wholly-owned and operated school, there was no problem with the law or the Authorities. Craig closed his school, they merged, and he joined Hudson's organization as President with Hudson as CEO.

R....RHINOCEROS.."You can't hit the side of a barn!" Maximilian the rhinoceros heard a hyena named Hermes say this to his girl friend, a hyena named Bitsie. Bitsie

RHINOCEROS..(CONTINUED)..Bitsie became angry and told Hermes: We're not throwing rocks at barns, we're throwing them at targets." "That's just a figure of speech," said Hermes."I would like to teach you to throw better." Bitsie calmed down and told Hermes she would like that.

Maximilian was the type of rhinoceros who had a nack for realizing and knowing when there was a need for something important and necessary. He sensed that hitting the side of a barn was important to many individuals.

He bought a barn and set up a stand near a road and put up a sign that read: "PRACTICE HITTTING THE SIDE OF A BARN! ONLY 10 JCs FOR A FULL PAIL OF ROCKS!" (JC is short for Jungle Currency) Individuals saw the sign and stopped their vehicles to talk to Maximilian.

They asked him what was so important about hitting the side of a barn. He, Maximilian,explained that the hitting itself was only part of a truly great and magnificent experience that gave

RHINOCEROS..(CONTINUED)..one a feeling of self-fulfillment and supreme accompishment. He orated at length about the supreme challenge that one confronted when he finally picked up a stone preparing to thrown it at the the side of the barn.

Many of the spectators bought a pail of rocks and went to throw them at the side of the barn; they did this to get away from Maximilian and his oration. But the idea was novel and individuals and birds were soon flocking to his stand.He decided to franchise his idea and set up barn-hitting places all over the jungle.

Barn-hitting mania swept the jungle; companies designed and built special barns for hitting purposes,and soon barn-hitting clubs sprang up through out the jungle. Professional barn-hitting teams were soon organized into leagues, and the teams ended the season with the Elgnuj Seires (Jungle Series spelled backwards) of barn-hitting.

The winning team won a gold silo-shaped trophy trimmed with platinum hay, and there was a sculpture of the

RHINOCEROS..(CONTINUED)..winning stone mounted   on the side of the trophy. The stones themselves became popular collectibles. Things went very well with the sport of barn-hitting   until residents who lived near the Agridiums (where the barn-hitting teams played) started complaining about the noise of the stones hitting the sides of the barns.

The residents formed a group called the Jungle Noise Abatement Society (JNAS) and elected a patas monkey as President. They started a class action suit against the National Barn-Hitting Professional Association (NBHPA). As a result of the suit all games were halted.

The JNAS met with the NBHPA to try the straighten out the situation for the benefit of both organizations, and they both agreed to binding arbitration. The arbitrator, a crocodile named Grace, considered the controversy for two days and called the parties together to give her decision.

She instructed the NBHPA to use

RHINOCEROS..(CONTINUED)..pillows instead of stones to hit the sides of the barns, and thus reduce the noise. The NBHPA obeyed the ruling and used pillows. A few members of the JNAS objected to the thumping sound when the pillows hit the side of the barns, and suggested using pillows without feathers.Grace rejected that idea. The NBHPA soon went international and became an even more popular sport.

S....SLOTH..Graham the sloth (two-toed) overheard two individuals arguing, and at the end of the argument one of them smiled and triumphantly said:"I have had the last word in this conversation.!" and walked away. The other one glared angrily,turned around, and walked in the other direction.

Graham considered this situation and went around asking every one if having the last word in a conversation was important to them. Every one he talked to said that getting the last word was of primary importance to them; they said it was the key to winning any argument or making any

SLOTH..(CONTINUED)..point. They said it was also important during debates.All of these comments impressed Graham, and he felt there was a need for education in this matter. He, therefore, founded the University of Last Words (ULW) to teach individuals how to have the last word in their various professions and activities.

The ULW was divided into Colleges of Politics, Science, Sociology,Cooking, Literature, and History. A spectacled bear named Declan was running for an office but was having problems with his speeches when he debated against other candidates.

He realized that getting in the last word in a speech was of great importance, but was sometimes unable to do this. He enrolled in the College of Politics at ULW and was assured that the courses he took would not only help him get the last word in, but would also improve his overall speechmaking ability.

In the Political Public Speaking 101 class,the professor told Declan to listen very carefully to what each candidate had

SLOTH..(CONTINUED)..to say and make a
mental note of the highlights of the
speeches. In Political Strategy 101 the
professor told Declan to pay absolutely no
attention to what the other candidates
said. In Basic Politics 101 the professor
told Declan to be against everything the
other candidates stood for whatever those
ideas might be.

In Advanced Politics 101, the
professor told Declan to ignore the other
candidates and discuss the major issues in
the election in extreme infinite detail
to the point where the voters will forget
the issues themselves. In Advanced
Political Strategy 101 the professor told
Declan to talk about subjects that have
nothing to do with the issues.

In Basic Political Strategy 101 the
professor told Declan that voters like to
hear about things that are familiar to
them and if he goes blank where he can't
think of anything political to say, he
should recite nursery rhymes.

Declan became very confused and
disgusted regarding all these different

SLOTH..(CONTINUED)..instructions and stopped all interviews, comments, speeches, and campaigning. He decided that he needed a vacation. He went on a world tour and was gone for a full four weeks before the election. He returned to his town the day after the election and was informed that he had won.

S....SERVAL..There was a crisis in the world of sports where it was necessary to use whistles. When a referee blew his whistle during a game, the players often didn't know what the signal meant. This happened over and over again, and disturbed the enjoyment of the game by both players and spectators.

It was also a factor during close games where there was a dispute as to the winner. Honorato the serval was watching a Swamp Wading Race and noticed that the players got confused when the referee blew his whistle. After much work and research, Honorato invented a whistle with a microchip that could be

SERVAL..(CONTINUED)..programmed to always give the right whistle signal at the right time. It was adaptable for a number of different sports. The whistle blowing signals for the following sports were as follows: BASKET COCONUT:..Free throws,Take it out, Foul, Need new coconut. VINE SWINGING:.Vine to short, Vine too long, Incorrect angle with tree, Swing too wide.

SAVANNA RACING:..Start, Quarter turn, Half turn, Three-quarter turn, Finish. DIK-DIK RACING:..Betting start, Betting Close, Win, Place, Show.SWAMP WADING RACE: ..Start, Caution, Resume, Finish. BACKWARD TREE CLIMBING:..Vertical start, Vertical time out, Vertical start again, Vertical finish.

Everything went well for a long time and Honorato's Microchip Whistle Factory was doing very good business; he, in effect, had a ready made market for his product.

Then, something happened; there was a production glitch at the factory and the chips were not installed correctly. They were not whistling correct signals for the

SERVAL..(CONTINUED)..correct situations
of the correct games. There was a great
deal of confusion: The dik-diks got the
Basket Coconut Free throw signal, and
stopped running and then started   to
throw coconut baskets;the Vine Swingers
stopped swinging on vines and started
wading through swamps;and the Savanna
Racers were climbing trees backwards.

The Basket Coconut players were
swinging through the trees on vines;the
Backward Tree Climbers were racing on
the savanna; and the Swamp Waders were
taking bets at dik-dik racing.

This was a real crisis for Honorato
and his whistle factory; something had
to be done. He called an emergency
meeting of all of his supervisors, and
they all agreed that the problem must be
a computer virus that had gotten into
the factory.

An ibis named Landa heard about the
virus problem at Honorato's factory and
contacted him. She told him that she had
invented a machine that she felt could
help him solve his problem. She told him

SERVAL..(CONTINUED)..the machine was called an Electro-Vacuum Computer Virus Confuser (EVEVC) which was guaranteed to solve the computer virus problem. They got together and discussed her machine. He said to her: "I assume your machine works on an electro-vacuum principle."

Landa said: "No, it works on an underheated steam principle, with the underheated steam being pushed against pieces of solid steel and then bombarded with sulfur atoms." "Then why do you have the words 'Electro-Vacuum' in the name of your machine?" asked Honorato.

"That's the reason for the word 'confuser' which is the basic principle of its operation.It is programmed for maximum security, so that not only the operators don't know what it's doing,but the machine itself doesn't know what it's doing. The mode of operation cannot possibly be in any way compromised," said Landa.

Landa used her machine to solve the virus problem for Honorato and he was back in business. He asked her what she charged and she asked for stock in his company; he

SERVAL..(CONTINUED)..gave her a thousand shares with an option to buy another thousand. Landa thanked him and they became very good friends.

S....SQUIRREL..Jetal the squirrel was watching a shampoo opera (he didn't like the soap kinds) and during an argument between two of the players one of them said: "It won't happen during a month of Sundays!" Jetal thought a month of Sundays would really be nice; it would be a situation that every one would enjoy.

Jetal decided to publish a calendar consisting of only Sundays. It would be a thirty-day calendar. He realized that to be successful in this endeaver he would have to get official government recognition for his idea. He applied to the Jungle Bureau of Time, Dates, and Calendars (JBTDC).

He gave the following speech to that body: "Think of the possibilities of a full month of Sundays! It would be a true time period or fun and pleasure! Citizens could go on vacations, camping, spas, and

SQUIRREL..(CONTINUED)..churches!They could do things around the house; visit friends and neighbors; have back yard barbecues; and enjoy tail gate parties. They could travel, visit relatives, and go to sports events.

They could do all the things they usually do on Sundays, every day of the month!"The Bureau members listened quietly and carefully. One of the members turned on her mike and said: "I'm Allura,a dama gazelle from the West Savanna District. Your idea is great! I'm sure every one likes the concept; it would be like every day being a holiday.

But there is a slight problem regarding your idea." "What's that?,"asked Jetal."When would every one work, and go to their jobs, and earn money if every day is a Sunday? " said Allura."I'm talking about citizens who normally work a five day week from Monday to Friday."

Jetal thought for a few seconds and said:"I admit that there are a few minor problems in my idea that should be addressed and worked out. What do you

WEIRD CONTEMPORARY FABLES

SQUIRREL..(CONTINUED)..usually do in this kind of situation?""We would, of course, send it to a committee, and since this involves the economy of the country, your proposition would be sent to the Committee For Jungle Economy and Welfare," said Allura.

"Suppose they can't solve the problem?" asked Jetal. "Then it goes to the Committee Concerning Problems that other Committees Can't Solve," (CCPOCCS)" said Allura."If there are still no results it will go to the Table Committee, who have a heavy duty, steel reinforced oak table for the purpose of tabling ideas and propositions."

"Does that mean my idea will be tabled?" asked Jetal. Allura smiled and said:" Not just tabled, Jetal. We're more organized and efficient than that. It will be tabled within a certain category.""What category is that?" asked Jetal. Allura smiled and said: "For consideration at a future date!"

"Who decides on those future dates?" asked Jetal. "The Committee For Future

- 197 -

SQUIRREL..(CONTINUED)..Dates of Tabled
Propositions (CFFDTP)," answered Allura.
"I have an important question, Allura,"
said Jetal."Should I continue publishing
my monthly calendar of all Sundays?" "Your
important question would go to the
Important Question Committee Involving
What to do Next (IQCIWN),"answered Allura.

"What if they can't come to a
decision?" asked Jetal. "Then it goes back
again to the Committee Concerning Problems
that other Committees Can't Solve(CCPOCCS)"
answered Allura. Jetal then said "What
happens next....never mind....I withdraw
that question!" He thanked Allura and the
rest of the members and ran out of the
room. He decided to only publish regular
calendars.

T....TAPIR..Dom the tapir was passing a
group of individuals who were talking and
he overheard one of them say to another:
"You like to do a lot of wool-gathering
don't you?" The other one answered:"Yes,
and I enjoy wool-gathering!." Dom asked a
friend exactly what wool-gathering means

TAPIR..(CONTINUED)..and his friend told him that it's similar to day-dreaming. Dom conducted a survey asking large numbers of individuals if they ever engage in wool-gathering; a very large majority said "yes", they did that at one time or another.

Dom opened up an establishment called the "Wool-Gathering Emporium,"a place where individuals could come to gather wool. There was five floors at the place, and each floor was of a certain category. The categories were about certain subjects.

"Wealth" was the first floor; "Travel" the Second Floor; "Fame"the Third Floor; "Exploration" the Fourth Floor; and "Invention" the Fifth Floor.

The Guest who came to the place would be given a basket and would walk around a room and gather chunks of the appropriate wool for the particular category. The guest would then go into a private room, close the door, sit back in a comfortable chair, and actually immerse himself or herself in the nice

TAPIR..(CONTINUED)..pleasant, intense, mentally realistic, and enjoyable feelings of wool-gathering. The room also had a panel with buttons, and each button had a label which showed sub-divisions of each category.

When a particular button is pushed, sub-division wool would come out of a chute to be added to the wool that already had been gathered. If a Guest came to the "Wool-Gathering Emporium" and wanted to do some wool-gathering about being wealthy, they would go to the "Wealth" first floor.

After going through the first procedure with the basket, and going into the room they would look at the buttons on the "Wealth" panel showing all the sub-divisions. Those sub-divisions would be: "Winning the Lottery;" "Investments;" "Real Estate;"and"Business Profitability."

If a Guest wanted to do some wool-gathering about "Travel," they would go to the "Travel" second floor. After going through the preliminary basic procedures, they would look at the"Travel" sub-divisions on the button panel. The

TAPIR..(CONTINUED)..sub-divisions would be: "North America;" "Europe;" "Asia;" and "Africa." The "Fame" buttons would have the following sub-divisions: "Literature;""Philosophy;" Politics;" and "History."

"Exploration" would have the following sub-divisions: "Arctic;" "Jungles;" "Deserts;" and "Forests." "Invention" would have the following sub-divisions: "Electronics;""Computers;" "Communications;" and "Construction." Dom, of course, charged for attending his "Wool-Gathering Emporium." There was a separate charge for each category.

There had been an empty building across from Dom's "Emporium," but one day he came to his place and saw a sign on that building that read: "Cotton-Gathering Emporium." Dom called his attorney and got a court injunction against the "Cotton-Gathering Emporium" on the grounds of the "Common Statute Law of Usual Use of Common Subjects and Designations."

The charge was that the procedure of

WEIRD CONTEMPORARY FABLES

TAPIR..(CONTINUED).."Gathering can only
apply to wool. The "Cotton-Gathering
Emporium" was shut down as was the other
"Emporiums" that sprung up including
"Silk-Gathering;""Linen-Gathering;" and
"Rayon-Gathering." Dom did very well
financially and made a lot of money and
opened up branches of his "Emporiums."

His business was so successful that
individuals were spending a great deal of
time wool-gathering at the "Emporiums;"
in fact everyday jobs and activities were
being ignored all over the country. Stores
closed; transit lines stopped running;
public services came to a halt; and many
factories stopped operating.

An emergency government investigation
was started to do something about Dom's
places. The government asked Dom to close
his "Emporiums" but he refused saying that
he had a right to operate his "Emporiums."

Dom did make the government an offer,
however: he said he would close down his
"Emporiums if the government paid him a
subsidy not to operate them.The government
agreed to this, Dom closed his places,

TAPIR..(CONTINUED)..and collected a non-operating subsidy.

W....WILDEBEEST..A wildebeest named Theo was listening and watching television when the news commentator talked about individuals going somewhere and wanting to "rub elbows" with celebrities and famous names.

Theo said to himself:"There must be some easy and convenient way to allow this kind of contact." He thought a while longer and an idea came to him! It was to put renowned celebrities in one place and let individuals rub elbows with them!

He looked around and found a large hall which he rented; he then configured it with parallel lanes of ropes. Famous celebrities called "Staff" would be on each lane to engage in elbow rubbing with guests who came to contact them.

There would be separate lanes for Politicians; Movie Stars; TV Stars; Stage Actors; Stage Actresses; Musicians; Explorers; and Scientists. The Staff members, would, of course be paid.

WILDEBEEST..(CONTINUED)..Theo called his place the "Elbow Rubbing Experience" Soon he got some competition. A wildebeest named Ajax opened up a place he called the "Shoulder Rubbing Palace," which was patterned along the same procedure as Theo's "Elbow Rubbing Experience," except that shoulders were rubbed.

The rubbing idea caught on fast. Soon other kinds of rubbing places opened up all over the country, and these included Foot Rubbing; Pinkie Rubbing; Thumb Rubbing; Big Toe Rubbing; Nose Rubbing;and Ear Rubbing. The situation was turning into a national fad and craze;"Happy Rubbing Day" became a standard greeting.

Things were getting somewhat out of hand, and the government was called uponto do something. The practice couldn't be banned completely because it wasn 't at all illegal, so the government took the next logical step: regulation and licensing.

The rubbing fad finally ended of itself because there were so many place doing it; the phenomena called "fracturing

WILDEBEEST..(CONTINUED)..the market" helped make it disappear. There were too many establishments for the number of guests in spite of the popularity of the rubbing fad.

W....WOLVERINE..Friends of Kyan the wolverine told him that they wanted to do certain things but were"on the fence." He knew what this meant: it meant they couldn't quite make up their minds about what to do and what kind of decisions to make in various situations.

Kyan got an idea: put up fences for individuals to be on. The fences would be custom-made to fit the individual's personal situation. He established a company to put up fences with a large area in back of the building. The fence was put up there and there was a chair mounted on the fence with half the chair on one side and half on the other side.

Kyan didn't sell these fences, but rented them out to customers and different customers could use them for similar purposes.Kyan gave the customers an hour on the fence for a fee. One

WOLVERINE..(CONTINUED)..day a customer came to Kyan's place and said he was "on the fence" as to where he wanted to go on vacation.Kyan had a "Vacation Fence" built where the customer was literally and actually "on the fence" deciding as to where he wanted to go. He finally came to a decision after an hour, paid the fee, and left.

Another customer came to Kyan's place and said he was "on the fence" with regard to investments; he couldn't decide how and where to invest his money. Kyan had an "Investment Fence" built for the customer who sat on the chair on the top of the fence for an hour.

After that he arrived at investment decisions, paid Kyan the fee, and went straight to his broker. He invested in stocks, bonds, mutual funds, and the money market. The customer became very wealthy. When the customer was near Kyan's place, and some one asked him how he became so wealthy, he would point at the fence and say "That's what did it!"

Another customer came to Kyan and

WOLVERINE..(CONTINUED)..also said he needed investment advice and decisions; Kyan put him on the "Investment Fence" and he became very rich. Kyan didn't know how or why that fence of his was causing so many investment successes, and he didn't care about the reasons.

Customers came from all over to sit on the "Investment Fence" and get rich, and Kyan was collecting fees that was making him wealthy. Kyan decided that he could make more money if he put up another "Investment Fence"; he made another one exactly like the original. A customer came and sat on it but didn't do well at all;he lost money.

"There's something about that first original fence that paid off for investors," said Kyan to himself."I'm going to find out what that is. It must be a certain something in the post or fence itself.If I can find it I can make lots of fences and really become rich."

He called the company that constructed the fence for him and told them to take it down and pull it apart.

WOLVERINE..(CONTINUED)..Kyan watched this procedure; he didn't know what he was looking for, but knew he would recognize it when he saw it. It took two hours to take the fence down, and Kyan couldn't find anything that looked like a part or mechanism that would cause correct investment decisions.

He told the fence workers to put the fence back up, which they did. After the fence workers left, a customer came to Kyan and wanted to sit on the "Investment Fence." The customer did this and did very badly investment-wise. All the customers after that using the "Investment Fence" were financially unsuccessful. The next day a flock of odd-colored geese flew over Kyan's place, swooping very low over the "Investment Fence."

W....WOODCHUCK..Dusty the woodchuck was reading history books with stories about one-horse towns. She came across many of them and started thinking to herself: Why do these towns have to continue being one-horse towns? Why can't they grow and become at least two-horse towns and maybe

WOODCHUCK..(CONTINUED)..even towns of more horses than that? An idea started forming in her head: Start a business selling expansion horses to one-horse towns! She did some research and then compiled a list of one-horse towns; that list turned out to be quite long.

She contacted all of them and got a good response, although a number of them said they enjoyed being one-horse towns and didn't need any more horses. She also talked to a number of horse breeders to arrange for a supply of horses.

Things went well for awhile but then some conflict arose. Dusty got a call from the mayor of one of the many one-horse towns that she had contacted. He told her that the town council had had a heated and loud debate concerning whether or not they wanted to become a two- or more horse town.

There was also meetings, banners, parades, and demonstrations. There was a conservative town faction that walked around with signs and placards reading

WOODCHUCK..(CONTINUED).."ONE HORSE IS
ENOUGH! The more liberal and progressive
faction went around with signs reading:
"THIS TOWN MUST GROW!WE NEED MORE HORSES!"
The mayor told Dusty that the situation
getting more serious all the time. He
asked her to come there and try to calm
things down.

Dusty felt that she should address
this problem, and went to the town where
she was met by the mayor.The next day she
appeared at a special meeting of the town
council, and as she stood up to speak the
conservative faction booed and jeered her.
The progressive faction cheered her. She
managed to calm every one down and asked
for quiet in the council chambers.

Dusty realized that the situation was
at an impasse, and suggested to the mayor
that the town have a referendum regarding
the horse matter. The mayor agreed, set a
date for the referendum, and after the
votes were cast the results were exactly
fifty-fifty, half for and half against the
horse question.

"What should we do now?" the mayor

WOODCHUCK..(CONTINUED)..asked Dusty. She replied: "Since the referendum was split half and half, then split the town half and half, with half the town staying a one-horse town and the other half getting more horses." "Exactly where will we split the town?" said the mayor.

"I notice that your town like many others has a Main Street," said Dusty. "Split the town on either side of Main." "Should we put some kind of a barrier there,so that every one knows where the split is?" asked the mayor. "Yes, we should", said Dusty."But we also should bear in mind that the two factions are still part of the town as a whole in spite of their differences, so the barrier should not be too offensive or formidable."

"What do you suggest?" said the mayor. "A six foot thick brick wall ten stores high," said Dusty."What about me?" said the mayor. "Would I continue to be mayor of the town as a whole.?"Which of the factions do you like?" said

WEIRD CONTEMPORARY FABLES

WOODCHUCK..(CONTINUED)..Dusty. "Do you
like the conservatives or the liberals?"
"I go for the liberals," said the mayor.
"Talk to them and see if they would accept
you," said Dusty. "What about you,"Dusty.
"What are you going to do now?" said the
mayor.

"I'll pack and go back to my home and
business," said Dusty. "Do you like this
town?" said the mayor. "Yes, I do, I like
it very much," said Dusty. "Which faction
do you like, said the mayor. "I go for the
conservatives," said Dusty. "They'll need
a mayor over there! Talk to them and see
if they will accept you as mayor for that
side of town!" said the mayor.

Both the mayor and Dusty became
mayors for their respective sides of the
town. Before Dusty assumed office, she
went back home and sold her horse business
to an equity group. Before buying Dusty's
corporation, the CEO of the equity group
asked her if her one-horse, two-horse,etc.
town had good future possibilities.

She said yes, and told them about the
expansion of one town into two,as a result

WOODCHUCK..(CONTINUED)..of the two factions.

Y....YAK..Horace the yak was a high excutive with a manufacturing company and worked in an office with a lot of other workers.Quite often he would hear a fellow excutive go into his office in the morning and say: "I'm not myself today." He also heard other individuals say this.

Whenever he heard some one say this a question came into his mind: "Who are you then?" He got the impression that some individuals would like to be some one other than who they are, at least on a temporary basis.This thinking gave him an idea: A place where some one could be some one else.

He rented a big building and built small one-individual booths, and each booth had a sign on the door: The signs on the door of each booth read as follows: "A GENERAL OF A BIG ARMY:" "AN EXPLORER FINDING NEW AREAS:""AN INVENTOR INVENTING THE ULTIMATE INVENTION:" "A MATHEMATICIAN SQUARING THE CIRCLE" "A

YAK..(CONTINUED)..NOVELIST WRITING A BEST SELLER:" and "A MUSICIAN WINNING NATIONAL AND INTERNATIONAL AWARDS."Inside the booth there was a chair and images were projected on the ceiling, the floor, and on each of the four walls.

The images concerning the signs on the doors were :The "General" booth showed marching soldiers and various weapons of war;the "Explorer" booth showed a scene of a dense jungle; the "Inventor" booth showed an inventor constructing a mysterious gadget; the "Mathematician" booth showed a professor writing equations on a blackboard; the "Novelist" booth showed an author at a typewriter; and the "Musician" showed a violinist.

Horace put a big sign on the building reading: "BE SOME ONE ELSE OTHER THAN YOU ARE!" Horace did a good business at his place with many patrons coming in to visit the booths. A yak named Merlin went up to Horace and said to him: ""What about patrons who are glad to be who they are?" "That's fine," said Horace."Let them be that way."

YAK..(CONTINUED).."Why don't you have a booth for them?"said Merlin. "There may many patrons who feel that way."Horace, who was, of course, charging patrons for the use of the booths, thought about what Merlin said. "I could attract more patrons by doing this," Horace said to himself.

He provided another booth for patrons who liked being the way they already are, and put a sign on that booth reading:"STAY JUST AS YOU ARE NOW." Patrons were encouraged to bring photos, collectibles, mementos, souvenirs, and other items of their past and present to put on the walls. ceiling, and floor of the booth.Statistics were kept by Horace to tally the popularity of the various booths;ninety-six percent of the patrons went to the "STAY JUST AS YOU ARE NOW" booth.

Z....ZEBRA..Argus the zebra overheard one of his friends call another friend "the last of the big spenders." Argus knew what the phrase meant: it was a sarcastic remark that referred to some

ZEBRA..(CONTINUED)..one who is frugal and tight with money. Argus thought to himself that it would be interesting to do a twist on that phrase and reward those kind of individuals. Then he got an idea for a business and competition concerning this saying.

He rented a building at a shopping mall and put the following sign in the window: "COME IN AND MAKE SOME MONEY BECOMING THE LAST OF THE BIG SPENDERS!" When participants came into the store they would line up in front of a booth. When they came to the agent inside the booth they would be charged a registration fee of one hundred and fifty dollars and given a hundred dollars in vouchers that could only be used in this competition.

They were then told to try to become "the last of the big spenders" by going to the many shops and stores at the mall and spending the vouchers.The participants had to adhere to the following rules: they could only spend a small amount at a time; they had to buy merchandise at at least ten different stores; they could only buy

ZEBRA..(CONTINUED)..merchandise of the soft goods category; and they had to do this within an eight hour day between the hours of nine A. M. and five P. M. They had to return to the store and check in by five P. M.

The last participant to return and check in was declared the "last of the big spenders" and would get a prize of one thousand dollars in cash spendable anywhere. The competition proved to be very popular and many participants came to Argus and his store to register, get the hundred dollars in vouchers; spend that amount; and try to win the thousand dollars.

One day all the participants were out spending the vouchers and the store was empty. Suddenly one of the participants raced into the store and to the agent. He said to the agent: "I'm the last one aren't I? The last of the big spenders?"

The agent was about to say "Yes" when another participant ran into the store to check in. He checked in after

ZEBRA..(CONTINUED)..the first one so he potentially became the "last of the big spenders."This second one was hoping to win the thousand dollars, but a third one ran in and became potentially the winner. Others came in and saw what was going on, so they decided to wait and let some one else check in, so they could be last and win the money.

As a result hundreds of participants stood around in the store waiting for others to check in so they could become the "last of the big spenders" and win the money. The crowds waited and waited and finally one of them suggested that they organize and form a club; he said that all of them might have a better chance of being last if they all got together as a group.

Many questioned the logic of this idea and couldn't figure out how this might happen, but many others couldn't resist the idea of organizing into a club. The organizing instinct is strong in many individuals.

A lot of them felt that they could

ZEBRA..(CONTINUED)..like the camaraderie
of this type of situation. They had a
meeting; elected officers; made up a
constitution; and appointed committees.
While this was going on, every one
in the club that was forming forgot about
the competition and winning the thousand
dollars.

   While all the club forming
activities were going on, a participant
ran into the store past the group and
checked in just at the closing time of
five P. M. He became the "last of the
big spenders" and won the thousand
dollars.

ISBN 142516116-2